SWINGS & ROUNDABOUTS

To Debbie

SWINGS & ROUNDABOUTS

Happy reading!

BETHANY RUTH ANDERSON

Bethany Ruth x

12·01·21

Bamboccioni Books

P.S I think I used to have a proper autograph - but I've forgotten how!

First published in Great Britain in 2013 by
Bamboccioni Books
15 Ravens Lane
Berkhamsted
HP4 2DX
www.bamboccionibooks.com

Swings and Roundabouts © Bethany Ruth Anderson 2013

The rights of Bethany Ruth Anderson to be identified as the author have been asserted in accordance with the Copyright, Designs and Patents Act 1988

A catalogue record for this book is available from the British Library

ISBN 9780956871718

All rights reserved. No part of this publication may be reproduced, transmitted, or stored in a retrieval system, in any form or by any means, without prior permission in writing from Bamboccioni Books.

Cover art by Phillip Bannister (www.nookiedesign.com)

Cover image © Sam Rose

Bamboccioni Books logo designed by Jennifer Abbot

(www.jcdizzystar.com)

For Mum, and for Owen,

for saying I would, and knowing I could.

ONE

Sarah

Ruby red or disco pink? This decision is beyond me. Ruby red or disco pink? What does each colour really say? Red: I am an assertive, intelligent woman who knows what she wants and gets it. Pink: a flirty and vivacious female who just loves having a great time. Who will I be tonight? Thick and dark, the paint oozes off the brush and gloops over my nails. Carefully, I pull the brush from cuticle to tip, aiming for a precision and skill that I don't have. A neat set of ten, they look more dirty mauve than anything else. Dark, mysterious; this will have to be my new game.

Finished, my palms rest on my knees, fingers spread apart so the nails don't stick. I've opted for a black knee-length dress. Hidden beneath opaque Lycra, my knees have definitely looked worse.

Vodka Bar. It seemed like a good idea at the time, something that a keen vodka lover shouldn't and couldn't stay away from. In fairness, the prospect of all the different colours and flavours excites me. Oh dear God, it's a Thursday night but the place might still be busy. There might be lots of really attractive people; young, slim, laughing, wearing the right clothes and drinking the right drinks. I pinch my thumb and forefinger together to make a pair of tweezers and use the rounded ends of my nails to pick at some stubborn fluff on my ankle. Fuck's sake. And then there's my cleavage. It's definitely real, and something I can occasionally boast about, but tonight they are too big, too round. The low round collar of my dress would look so much better on Lisa; a skeletal frame which every material clings to. Sometimes it seems that clothing loves her, enjoys being draped across her pointed collar bone and prominent hips.

Okay; phone, keys, wallet, passport... Good to go. Pink plastic cuckoos tweet eight times from their clock house: fifteen minutes late. So much for sixty second miracle dry.

Emerging onto the street I look up and down the pavement. There aren't so many people around. It's a week day and cars are muted across wet roads. The street lamps do their best to light my way but the darkness threatens to snuff them out. Pressing the button for the green man I feel the metal scraping across the thick coat of ruby red. Shit. It's difficult to examine the scale of the damage beneath the flickering pelican crossing. What if somebody sees it? What if I get to the bar and hand over my money and someone sees the dent on my middle finger? My cover would be blown. No more stylish, *au fait* city girl. A couple of girls walk just ahead of me, slowing me down. Their arms are linked together as they keep each other up, two clowns on stilts. Daringly, I glance at the reflection of my feet in a shop window. Steady on my heels, almost. The November rain is pathetic, barely a drizzle, but I dip my head anyway, worried about the potential damage it could cause my hair.

'Sarah?'

Lisa calls me over from outside the bar. She's lingering with some guy I've never seen before; he's too short for her to be possibly interested in him but, for now, his goofy smile continues to be a source of amusement.

'Hi Lisa.'

Again this random guy is scrutinised. I don't like his bad haircut and I don't appreciate the fact that he smokes. Is that why she's standing out here?

'Since you were late I just thought I'd wait outside for you for a bit.' She shakes her head slowly, a discreet finger motioning towards the smoker. She chose disco pink.

'Okay, let's just go get something to drink.'

I can't grab her arm quick enough as I pull her inside. Not so fast. Rummaging through my tiny bag I seek out my passport; I always bring it, readily available. There's just no point getting embarrassed or pissed off any more. Maybe when I'm forty I'll look twenty so it'll be okay.

Sweat mingles with the sweet scents of the cocktails in the bar. Everyone is drinking something pink, orange, green or even blue. The blue one is dubious: it's slightly worrying that something that colour is even drinkable. Still, whatever it is excites me so I ask for 'the blue one' when we order at the bar while Lisa just smiles and says, 'Woo-woo for me, please'. I don't know how many times I've watched her bar etiquette. She drapes herself over the bar, a pose that I can't mimic because my breasts rest on the menus and I look like some kind of whore. Her skinny fingers walk across the napkin that's been placed in front of her and she fingers a black straw, the end sitting on glossy lips. I pout in red and feel like a fish, sure that people are rolling their eyes at the girl trying to get attention. But no one looks at Lisa like that. No one laughs at a model, no one laughs at a girl who is worth a second glance. Beside her, I can feel those long second looks from eye across the room. I dip my head, hiding in the periphery.

Matt
Fuck knows what that shit was. Porridge and vodka? Who came up with that idea? Fucking wrong, that's what it is. But that's the fun isn't it. It's wrong, disgusting. The picture on the drinks menu has a skull and crossbones. It's not like it's poison, for fuck's sake. Not that he knows what poison tastes like. Or does he? Holy shit, Johnny's buying five more. Fuck off, Johnny.

'Johnny, fuck off. Get me a strawberry one.' Strawberry shot - tastes like Calpol. Like the good old days when they went to the pharmacy. One for Matt, one for Johnny. Let's drink some Calpol, boyo. Maybe it didn't even make them high but it was legal so they did it. Cool kids on campus. No thank you, sir, we don't care for your heroin. Weed? Nah, we have our stuff. Stuff. Yup, this tastes just like Calpol. Five times over and it still tastes like Calpol, but he tastes the vodka now. He feels the vodka now.

'Aw man, we love this song!' Johnny is way too excited. Vodka always gets to him. Matt doesn't even know the tune and he's sure Johnny doesn't either. They dance anyway. Johnny's already gyrating behind a couple of girls. Haha, what a dick. He's dancing like some kind of gay boy. Like George Michael or Michael Jackson. Creepy. Edging through the crowd from the bar, Matt finds him eventually. He laughs because he's in complete dismay at his friend's big fish, small fish, moonwalk routine. But Johnny's dancing isn't interesting anymore anyway, cause there are two really hot girls at the bar. One is too skinny. She's hot and she knows it, sucking on the end of her straw. Pass. Her friend loiters, like she doesn't want to be here. Nice legs, modest dress. Is she trying to copy her friend? It doesn't work. Looking like a rabbit caught in headlights, wide eyes, panicked, ready to run. She *really* doesn't want to be here. Hot but doesn't know it. Like it.

'Hey.' Her friend is busy with some other guy. Matt offers to buy her a drink even though she just got one. An apologetic smile and she politely declines with a little shake of her head. Her hair is nice and wispy.

'No problem! You dance?' She repeats the motion. Guess it's okay cause he doesn't dance either. Well, not here. Not like Johnny. Not like JT over there.

'Okay.' Tugging at his tie, thinking what to say. This isn't a conversation. She doesn't speak. Maybe she can't. Matt thinks the look that he gives her is too suspicious because now she's giving a worried smile. Her lips part - nice teeth - but her eye-shadowed eyes look scared. He's no wolf, he won't gobble her up. Okay, maybe. Not now. Not tonight. Maybe.

'So... I'm going out for some fresh air. Coming?' Matt cocks his head towards the door and she puts her half-empty pink drink on the bar.

'Okay.' Her first word. Well done. Congratulations. Least she can speak, would be pretty weird if she couldn't. But maybe kind of cool. Girls talk such shit.

'Nice.' Leading the way, he battles through drunkards. Did they have eight shots too? Hell, yeah! Those were good. Outside is really fucking cold and it's raining heavier now. The rain falls in straight lines in front of the light from the street. Shit. Better get a taxi home. This is what smoking areas are good for. Bars are always providing tents or umbrellas for the cancer sticks.

'Having a good night?' He knows she's not, but whatever.

'Yeah. It's nice in there.' She's lying and her eyes look

back towards the door, shit music blaring, reaching us out in the rain.

'Yeah.' They stand awkwardly in mutual agreement of something that they're both lying about. 'Actually...this place is shit. Drinks are good, but I hate it here.'

That broke the ice. Her smile looks more genuine now and her shoulders relax. God, she must have been tense. She has a nice laugh. It makes Matt take another look at her.

'I don't like it either. I just came with my friend.'

Her friend must be the skinny one.

'Me too. Johnny loves shit R'n'B nights.' He does too sometimes, but whatever. Only on rare occasions. Today is not a rare occasion. Her dress is a little too big for her. Looks nice across her boobs though.

'Mmhmm, so does Lisa.' She wraps her arms across her stomach and she looks really nervous. Matt thanks God that he's not in his intense mode. He could be. That would be funny. She'd just run away.

'Maybe Lisa and Johnny should hook up.' Matt says it more to himself cause he thinks it's pretty funny to be honest because Lisa and Johnny are pretty much two entirely different species of human being but he'd probably do her anyway. 'Damn, too late.'

Skinny Lisa stumbles past the bouncers, some gormless gargoyle holding her up.

'Oh my *God*! *Sarah*! There you are! Me and Andy are getting a taxi so share one with us, okay?' She's screeching way too loud.

This girl, this Sarah, she's looking at Matt like she doesn't really want to get in a taxi with them. But she tiptoes round some puddles to get to Lisa. Here comes the taxi. Jack Daniel's taxi. His personal favourite. She's not going to ask him to come too.

Taking hold of Skinny Lisa's other arm, this Sarah lifts a hand and waves at Matt. 'See you later,' she says. She says that, but she probably won't.

TWO

Matt

He still doesn't know why he has this job. Okay, so Dan was shagging some fat goth that works there, and pulled some strings (or g strings) and voila, Matt the barman. But why did he take it? Shift's not even started yet but he really doesn't want it to. What's that Mr. Manager, sir? Oh dear, you lost your license for selling to some jailbait? Oh no! I'll have to leave? Ah well... No chance. Not 'no chance' that the bar's been serving under-agers, just no chance. Good stuff like that doesn't happen to Matt.

'Shifted those kegs yet?' He can't stand that grating Liverpool accent, the way it seems to pull at the insides of his ear.

'Yeah, all sorted. No problem.' He's being too nice, but that's the game that he plays. At least it makes his manager fuck off and leave him be. The shit Casio watch that he found on a club floor the other night blinks at him. Starting time.

There's always the same sad trio of old men that come in. They're like the cast-off skins of Iggy Pop or Axl Rose, wrinkly pale tattoos and heroin scars. Three JD and cokes, but later they'll pretend that it's a bit of a laugh to have a few tequilas. They mean no harm, despite their comments and jibes about the female customers. Matt's job is to remain impassive: join in when they want, disappear behind the bottles when they're being particularly bitchy. Hey, that's fair enough. What would they do without their favourite local?

'Hey boys, it's our pal, the skinny black haired yin.'

'Aw, here, ah thought ye meant the lassie!' They laugh, making the same shitty jokes that they always do. Oh ha ha, bar guy tonight. Not the bar maid. Though it would be nice to have a shift or two with her. Oh yes, it would.

'So what can I get for you ladies this evening?' Just playing along with the lady jokes. Matt wears his winning smile, safe in the knowledge that if they were a group of women their hearts would be instantly won over.

'The usual, handsome.' Brittle brown teeth grimace and it's obvious that this isn't Iggy's first drink of the night. They're the only ones who actually ever order 'the usual'. These two girls, they come in and ask for the same thing every single time. A raspberry Absolut and lemonade. A Sailor Jerry's and coke. But they never ask for 'the usual.' Maybe they think Matt doesn't remember. But he forgives that; they're sweet, and they probably don't remember him anyway.

For at least an hour, the old Motley Crue are the only people in the pub. Leaning over the bar, Matt stretches to try and catch any of the fireworks that are blasting off around the city. Sounds like a war film, like footage on the news.

'Surprised ye arnae up the Seat startin' fires, pal.' Axl's milky eyes blink at Matt from over the top of his glass, the ridged edge reflecting his hairy nose several times.

Laugh. He really does laugh, and he readily admits, 'Believe me, I would be if I wasn't stuck here. Completely forgot what day it was.' Somehow when Dan and Sue asked him to work November 5th, he didn't remember, remember gunpowder, treason and plot. 'And anyway, who's to say I won't go up there when I'm done here?'

In unison, the men roll their eyes. Together they're worse than old ladies who chatter over tea. Best leave them to disapprove of his antics in a grandfatherly way and reminisce over the better pranks they played 'in their day'.

Matt's twenty-third bonfire night. Probably, it's the first time in seventeen years that he hasn't set fire to something. Apart from *those* years, obviously. Fireworks and gun powder aren't necessarily outlined on the list of things forbidden in the hospital but, like alcohol and mirrors, he was pretty sure they would be denied. Access to life denied. 'Sorry, mate, it's for your own good,' they said. 'Mate?' Matt wasn't sure he remembered being even remotely friendly with those people. Trying not to think of the white and the bleach and the therapy and the way his psychologist's hair parted in the middle. The pint glasses suddenly look in need of shining.

'Matt, you can do the morning shift for me tomorrow, yeah?' He doesn't even get the chance to mutter anything more than a groan before Liverpool says, 'Good.' Not even 'thanks'. Fuck you, then. We'll just see if your pub is open for business tomorrow morning. He wasn't sure that he actually did mornings, especially not after a night of burning stuff; a mini attempt at an invisible parliament. After all, he hasn't been on a decent pyro rampage in a while. Maybe because there's no longer a constant supply of matches in his coat pocket, but that's how it is now.

It's not in the least bit surprising that locking up starts so early. Only midnight and the pub is empty, dead but for the Hello Kitty doll that Sue propped up against the Sourz bottles. Maybe it is *kinda* cute with its sad little tartan skirt. 'See you later, Kitty.'

The keys rattle in his jeans pocket and, even though they jingle with every couple of steps, at least it means they're definitely still there.

Arthur's Seat, and it looks like this party is over. Some dying embers fizz at scattered spots across the grass. Over rocks and empty bottles, used up rockets and sparklers, eventually he reaches the top. Spread beneath his feet is an entire city. Orange and white lights shine for miles and miles around, the only gap being a river in the distance.

'This city is mine!' Matt spins: shit, there's someone behind him. But it's just another firework, whimpering its way up into his sky, illuminating a green cityscape for just a second. Missed the best bonfires, missed the brightest rockets. Further away, red streaks twist into the darkness before melting into smoke. Sirens wail through hidden streets, too many fires, not enough engines. Sorry Sam.

This rock is cold and hard but there's a small hole to use as a fire pit. Clumps of grass and old receipts form the basis of his spectacle, and from the depths of his pocket appears the purple lighter that was left on one of the tables. There was a twenty pence piece there too, but this is definitely more useful. On top of the world, it is difficult to get a good flame from a lighter, and it doesn't help that this is apparently a pound shop affair.

At last! There is light! A cute little fire, flickering sporadically between breaths of wind. Matt's arms outstretch like some kind of poor man's Cristo Redentor. If the world is flat, then he is on the edge of it. It's all darkness and lights, all noises and silence. Laughter escapes from his chest, but it's so loud that he's not really sure where it came from, like his diaphragm is working overtime. 'I am Matthew James Cairns, ruler of creation and destruction.'

The need to yell at the world, slow and small, crawling beneath his feet, is overwhelming.

Master of the Universe. Fuck you He-Man, the world doesn't need you anymore.

THREE

Sarah

The needle flickers, anxiously fluctuating between two numerals. Maybe the point is connected to the speed of my heartbeat, so fast it blurs. What? The point of the needle stops, wobbling as it rests next to the eight figure. *What?* But...how? My feet retreat quickly onto the tiled bathroom floor, toes wriggling as they touch cold. Okay. Try again. But first, this time, I remove my towel and dump it over the bath; it *is* pretty heavy. Right foot. Left foot. My eyes meet a reflection in the steamed mirror. It's me, airbrushed by the white heat. Watching myself smile, no blemishes from where I'm standing. The spots around my nose and forehead have disappeared, the heavy purple bags beneath my eyes have vanished. Time to practise my smile, turning my face to find the nicest angle. My profile is best when viewed from the right. Wide, heart-grabbing smile; my teeth shine white beneath the bathroom light. Oh, hello. Why yes, I am free this Saturday. Why do you ask? A date? Oh, I'd be flattered. My hands touch at my cheeks to hide a coy blush that isn't really there. But my fingers don't reach high, flattering cheekbones. Instead they prod at flabby handfuls of fat. I want to blame my dad. Or Grandma. Not sure who is more to blame. I can't look at the reflection anymore so I don't know if the smile is still in the mirror, or if it's been replaced with something more sinister, something ugly.

Back to the scales. Between my feet - toes are in need of a good pedicure that I won't be able to afford - the needle... It's still at eight and it's not going to move. Not unless I remove my right foot and let it hover slightly. If I balance just right... Fuck it! My right foot kicks hard at the scales, sending them across the floor. They clatter on the blue stone tiles so my cursing is quiet - don't want to make any more of a scene than I already have. Just in case...

'Sarah! You okay in there?'

So much for keeping a low profile.

'Haha, yeah, fine! Just tripped over the stupid scales!' She laughs at me through the door; she believes the story because it's exactly the kind of clumsy thing I'd do.

My clothes are sitting in a pile on the mat beneath the sink, but deodorant has to go on first. It needs to dry properly before I put on my black work blouse, otherwise I'll spend the day paranoid about sweat stains or licking my fingers to rub away white lines that stretch across my ribs. The spray goes on 12cm away from my underarms, as directed. The blue and white canister boasts being unbeatable on white marks. It might be unbeatable but that doesn't mean that it actually works. Black bra, black blouse, black pencil skirt. Maybe Laura thinks I'm some kind of secret goth. Or maybe she doesn't care. Anyway, the bright pink costume jewellery that hangs at my neck and dangles on my earlobes proves otherwise. I like to think that it proves otherwise.

'You okay?' Naomi peers in the bathroom door, sipping tentatively from a cup of coffee that will have milk and two sugars in it.

An off-hand laugh and a flippant wave of my hand, 'Yeah. Just being clumsy again.' It's all just a big funny joke, my ability to make a disaster out of a simple mistake. Only, kicking the scales wasn't a mistake.

'Sorry. Thought I'd pushed them back under the sink. So's they were outta the way, y'know?' Her American boyfriend is making her speech lazy and slurred.

'Nah, it's okay.' Don't want her to feel bad. 'I'm still alive.' But if she's taking her diet seriously she could at least invest in some decent scales. If Naomi stepped on the scales right now, where would the needle point? The prospect of the figure 11 makes me feel queasy so I duck into my bedroom, quick and brisk like anyone getting ready to leave for work.

Smoky eyes or light and neutral? Enough of a goth as it is, my reflexes reach for the neutral palette. This pink colour barely shows on my eyelids but has enough of a shimmer that it's just noticeable. Just a little bit of eyeliner today. I hate getting tired and rubbing my eyes and going home to find lines of kohl stretched beneath my eyelashes, darkening the purple circles. Deep purple turns to lavender when I dab on thick liquid concealer. The blusher brush spreads pink powder across my cheeks, defining cheekbones that aren't there to highlight. Still, as I'll sit beneath flickering tube lighting all day, the pink will accentuate the features that I pretend to have. My eyes wander over the palette of lip gloss. But there's no need for juicy redness because there's no one to impress, not even myself. But I need maximum lashes. No clumping - not true. £15 and it does the same thing as the £3 budget deal. But who feels good in anything cheaper than Max Factor?

'Sarah! It's nine already!' Naomi's voice sounds panicked as it bursts through the space between my door and the frame. Someone stares back at me, face surrounded by a circle of pale round bulbs. The face looms forward and flinches then sits back and grimaces. I just can't get this right.

'I'm not going to work! I feel sick!' My hand finds its way from the purple vanity case to my stomach, squeezing tight at a fistful of flesh. The mirror girl mouths the words back at me. Copycat. Blinking, we begin a painful staring competition and I start to feel like a bad actress in a bad video for a Christina Aguilera song. I can't help but notice that Naomi's shoe appears in that gap by my door.

'Sarah, you're fine. And you look great, okay? That necklace is super nice. Cosy night in tonight, remember? It'll be nice.'

The prospect of staying in with Naomi, getting fat together on the sofa makes the nausea more real.

'Might just go to Lisa's tonight.' Skinny Lisa. Safe Lisa.

By now I have my black pea coat and houndstooth handbag at the ready.

'Oh...' Digging through my bag, the noise of my rummaging through keys, wallet, the bulk of my makeup bag, a mirror, brush, and phone drown out her disappointment.

'Okay. I don't know. Just might. I'll text you, yeah?' Pulling open the door, Naomi looms into full view, set and ready for her day's work at the zoo, her hair pulled back into a ridiculous ponytail. But then I've slipped past her and I'm calling to her as I fumble with the chain at the door. 'Have a good day!' An empty sentiment to settle any awkwardness that might affect our evening.

I hate mornings like this. Wake up and it's dark, come home and it's dark. Black and grey. Grey and black; so fed up of all the predictable monotony. Beside me the name Amy Mitchell is scribbled onto the button at the traffic lights. Who is Amy Mitchell and why did she feel the need to write her name in permanent marker, her 'i' dotted with a bubble heart? Green man and I can cross the road. Flora

Laura is standing in the shop window, rearranging some winter flowers in a vase. It's a much nicer display than some she's had before - pink roses and carnations and a purple flower that I want to say is lisianthus. Learning the names gradually, but then it's not really my job to know; all just wisdom that Laura feels the need to pass on to her secretary.

'Morning Sarah!' She stands back from her work, hands akimbo as her head tilts. It's her concentration stance. Her glasses slip to the end of a bulbous nose and she stares hard at all the colours. First she looks at them straight, then she crosses her eyes until the flowers fuzz - all the better to see how the colours *blend*. The ritual is repeated after every arrangement, much to the horror of the innocent bride-to-be or the melancholic mourner.

'Hi Laura.' I pass through the thickly scented jungle to reach the "office" and dump my bag beneath the desk, simultaneously reaching for the power button on the CPU. 'Tea or coffee?' My voice just about makes it through to the shop but I'm already in the adjoining kitchen filling the kettle with water. Laura is going to ask for tea because she always does at this time in the morning. Coffee is reserved for busy afternoons or late evening stock takes. While the kettle whistles to a boil I take a peek at my workload for the day. Twenty orders over the weekend- not too bad. Double click. The number of cheesy messages to go with the bouquets are embarrassing. *To my darling flower, some roses for a rose, but you always smell sweeter. Happy Birthday, love from Jack xxx* Even if someone took it upon themselves to ever buy me flowers, I know for sure that I would *not* be impressed by such a ridiculous message. But my opinions don't count here; it's just my handwriting on the card.

'Here you go.' Her Flower Fairies mug goes on the matching Flower Faeries coaster by the till. A little fairy at the bottom left hand corner is looking worse for wear. She's brown with caffeinated drops and her plastic legs are beginning to curl. Mental note: think about getting Laura a new coaster set for Christmas.

'Thank you, love.' Her smile twitches nervously as she eyes the mug before turning back to the window, 'How do you like the Christmas display?'

'Yeah, it's really pretty.' In all honesty, it's one of her better attempts.

And the compliment seems to have been enough because she walks with a more confident stride across the shop, feet silent in her worn sandals.

'Good.' She draws the word out far longer than necessary, and figuring she's finished I head back to my own tea. 'You know, I didn't want to go for the usual red and greens. It'd be nice to appeal to all the other religions too. You know, for the Pagans and the Jews as well.'

'Oh...uh huh. Yeah, that's nice.' Trust Laura to be thinking about everyone. It wasn't a business head that made her do it, just a soft brain cushioned by a mass of curls. Not really sure what Laura believes in, or even what she thinks she does. Dream catchers adorn the toilet cupboard but on her desk is a calendar featuring various seraphim and cherubim, a different angel quote for every day of the year. Pretty sure it's stuck on August 5 and, knowing Laura, it's probably because she particularly liked the look of that angel, or the sentiment of those specific words. The incense is burning already near the bathroom; not the cinnamon apple scent any customer would expect in December but a musky, heavy smell that isn't in my memory to recollect or name. She also has a strange habit of following the name Muhammad with a humble 'peace be upon him', though he doesn't find himself the regular topic of conversation.

'We got twenty orders, Laura.' I disappear into my cubbyhole intent on getting busy with today's mundane messages and revolting rhymes. It amazes me what people imagine will sound nice as an accompaniment to a bunch of flowers.

Happy Birthday, love from Mark. I don't feel so stupid writing down Mark's message

FOUR

Matt

She's adjusting her dress, pulling at the flimsy sequined material. But by tugging it further down over her hips she's revealing more of that chicken-fillet cleavage, which Matt's really not interested in. She doesn't have a name.

'Look, I really need to try and find my friend. He's had too much to drink and -'

Clearly she's not interested in any excuses. Yes, Johnny is drunk but he has no desire to find him. And he wouldn't appreciate being hounded while he's hot on the tail of some doped-up blonde. So Matt's still there, hands held high in defence.

'Aaaaasowhat?' Her words slur together as she tries to balance against a wardrobe, the cheap Ikea doors rattling on their screws.

'So I'm going.' End of. He's outta this scene. But there's a weight at his back, a hand on his shoulder stopping him from leaving. Oh God, it's her, and Matt's the leaning post. He can feel his gums pull back into a grimace as she leers, teetering on heels that are higher than necessary.

'Don' go away. Stay here. Stay here. With meeeeee.' Guessing that the face she is pulling is supposed to be her seduction mask.

Take one step away, one giant leap for his sanity. But she stumbles as Matt moves. He doesn't care where she lands, but her fall is broken by his chest. Why me? Willing to bet there are loads of sad guys downstairs who would give a limb for some time with a drunken drugged-up slag. No thanks. Hey, at least he has room for manners. It's so hard to straighten up without letting her fall on her face, so pushing her is definitely the easiest option.

She's on the floor now, a withered heap, and her nectarine face is moving closer to his crotch. Pretty sure she's trying to say something but she's bleating, neighing in her zebra print dress. Grabbing at his belt buckle. He thinks she's trying to stand. Well she can fuck off, that Batman buckle is precious.

'Heeeey.' She sounds more offended than wounded, staring with glassy eyes from her pile on the carpet. What the fuck is she doing holding onto his ankles?

'Get the fuck off me!' Shit. Someone's running up the stairs, towards the source of the scream. No one comes in, the noise was probably muffled by the heavy bass beat. Loud and obscure Ministry of Dance, Shit Anthems II or whatever they're playing. Matt doesn't hit women, never has, never would. It's like the unwritten golden rule of being a guy. Women are weaker, generally, but when provoked they make straight for the balls - it's a grave error to get in a fight with a girl. More important, it's hardly worth boasting about. He could have punched her, knocked her dead cold. Maybe folk would think she's passed out. But his dignity is scraping the bottom of the barrel as it is, so there's no way he'd even try it. Right now though, things look bad. She's lying on the floor, sprawled in a manner that's hardly ladylike, head close to a leg of the bed, hair all tangled around the wood. In 100% honesty, he didn't hit her. She grabbed at him, he moved sideways, and she fell. But Matt looks like the culprit in a bad version of Cluedo: Matt, in the bedroom, with bare fists. No chance.

Heading down the stairs, he's sure someone will find her, assume it's all just some accident. Under the affluence of incohol and all that. Where's Johnny? Matt doesn't know about 98% of the people here. Doesn't even know whose house this is. Rummaging through the fridge, ignoring bottles of beer and cider in the hunt for food. A half-eaten Pepperami. Eurgh, spitting the obviously stale 'meat' into the iced sink. He's still keeping his eyes peeled for Johnny. But if he's fucked off with that blonde, he's not gonna see him any time soon. The bastard's supposed to be driving them home. That plan has failed. Couldn't even wait to get the girl home. Dick. He really needs to get out of here.

'Oh, hey, need a drink?' Wow, she's hot, if swaying just a little on her feet, but Matt shakes his head politely, flashing that winning smile.

'Oh.' Heh; she seems pretty put out.

'Not drinking tonight.' Matt regrets the decision to stick by the rules on the packet, but he'd regret it even more in the morning if he didn't. Probably?

'Okay.' Using the bottom of a bottle, she's shifting through the ice in the sink to avoid getting chewed Pepperami on her hand.

'Who do you know here?' One hand is keeping her propped up against the counter while the other works hard with a bottle opener.

'Eh...not anyone, to be honest. Just came along with a friend.'

'Yeah, me too.' Sipping at her Peroni, she nods across the kitchen to a tall and skinny thing; she's laughing, but the guys buzzing around her haven't got the joke. Then again, maybe they weren't listening, paying her more attention with their eyes.

'Huh...' Bored now, and really not in the mood for a heart to heart. Although, eyeing Peroni girl over again, he's sure he can spare some time.

She's looking at him now, pretty little smile showing behind the green neck of her bottle, 'So... have a good night last weekend?'

What the fuck? Does he know her?

Sarah

He's looking at me like he doesn't recognise me. Or maybe that's just the way he looks under the flickering kitchen light. At least, I'm pretty sure that it's flickering, and it's not just the way that I'm squinting at it. 'You know, the other night? Or...maybe it was the other week? At the Vodka Bar.' The last bit isn't a question because the last bit I know for definite. I did meet him there. It's not a trick of the light.

'Oh...right, yeah, of course.' He's looking round the room, like he's looking for an excuse. But he's smiling and sounds like he at least might vaguely remember. It's nicer to pretend that he does anyway.

'Want a drink?' There's a bunch of bottles in some melting ice in the sink and some kind of sausage that someone spat in there. It's just gross. But he says no so I don't have to put my hand back in there, which is good, because I spent a long time painting my nails Red Carpet red. For the festive season. Apparently it's the in thing. I didn't really want to do the "in thing", I wanted to do my thing, but Lisa told me that green nail varnish was just teenage and stupid. She knows better than the magazines.

'Eh, no thanks.' Oh good, he's trying to remember. He ends in that abrupt way that suggests he's fishing for my name.

He's gonna get it. 'Sarah.'

How could that pretty face forget me? How could those

icy blue eyes forget that they ever looked upon me? Probably, he wouldn't, maybe, not if I wasn't standing next to Lisa all night, like a weird game of spot the difference.

His smile oozes honesty and promises, 'Matt. Nice to meet you. Again.'

'So... you don't know anyone here?'

'Just my mate Johnny. No idea where he is now though.' His shoulders move up and down, rolling into a shrug, and I can't help but notice the nice, gentle slope they make. They're strong shoulders and if he ever let me, which I'm sure he never would, I bet I'd be safe up there, even at my size. He looks like he could carry my weight, all of me, on his shoulders.

'Who does he know here? I mean, who invited him?' Just keep the questions rolling. So long as I'm asking him questions he can't just walk away, and the more conversation we have the more he'll *have* to remember me. This time.

He's hiding now, kneeling on the floor as he's rummaging through cupboards for...something. Leaning out from behind the wooden door he looks up at me, eyes hidden by an unruly fringe. 'Ehm... something... Callum? Or... Craig?'

'Callum Craig?' I catch myself giggling into the top of the bottle, my breath making noises down the neck.

'That's the one.' He returns to the marble co
tin of pineapple slices and now he's looking for
I'm guessing. But it's got one of those ring pull
While he's searching I take the tin, using shiny red talons to pull it open. Ouch. It bends my nail back, the nice rounded index finger nail. But it's worth it for the stupid smile that twitches on his lips.

'There you go.' Sliding the tin along to where he's pulling everything out of a drawer.

'Oh...' A pretty, stupid smile. He's already armed with a fork and he digs in, swallowing a couple of chunks before tipping the can towards me in offering.

'No thanks.' He sticks to his pineapple, I stick to my beer.

The tin is empty and Matt moves the fork around the inside like he's stirring a cup of tea. His foot is tapping and he's rolling his eyes. I don't really agree with the change of song either. 'Listen, this is really shit. I'm going for a walk. Coming?'

Wow. 'Oh, okay, yeah. Sure. Let me grab my stuff and tell Lisa.' Really, a walk anywhere with anyone would be more exciting than this. I don't know anyone here. I awkwardly lean through the barrier of lechery to reach Lisa, tapping her clammy bare shoulder.

'Sarah! There you are! Where did you go?' She winks at one of the guys before she looks at me and I have no idea why she does that. Whatever, if they were already talking about me or something, that's just another reason to leave.

'I'm going for a walk and I don't know if I'll be back.'

'Okay. Just text me when you get home safe, okay?' Well, if she didn't care enough to ask who with, at least she cared enough to ask me to text.

'Sure.'

Thank God. I don't know how Lisa does it, standing in the actual centre of attention like that. I don't know how she can tolerate those leering looks. They're like a pack of dogs slavering after some treats. Gross. And humiliating. Where's my jacket? I'm sure it was somewhere near... Aha! Matt's right behind me when I turn round, wrapped up in a black coat and a red tartan scarf. Very nice, very cosy.

'Ready. Lead the way.' I pull my arms into my winter jacket as I trail behind him out of the house, 'Where do you want to walk?'

'Need to figure out where we are first.'

Out of the flat, it's freezing outside; searching deep in my bag for my gloves, moving into the lamplight to get a better look at what I'm doing. Successful, the mittens are retrieved and pulled on. Matt's half way down the street by now, his eyes staring midway up the blocks of flats, looking for a street name.

'Eh... Sarah.' Matt motions to me from the bottom of the street, waving a hand. 'Meadows down this way.'

Walking side by side with Matt through the Meadows. Matt... 'So... Matt. What do you...do?' A lame, empty question. How boring and uniform. Hardly the exciting conversation that I bet he's used to.

The toe of a scuffed Converse shoe kicks at a stone, sending it tumbling down onto the road. 'Work in a pub most days. You?'

'Working in a florist's. It's not so bad. Just answering phones and emails, getting the orders together for delivery, that kind of thing.'

'Huh.'

'And...what do you do in your spare time? Weekends?' I'm spouting shit but I know it's the Peroni. And bad chat is better than no chat. I think.

'Photography, a bit. I like music, reading, films, the usual.' His head is tipped back and he doesn't really seem with it, as if his eyes are acting like little cameras, taking in the frosted branches and the stars.

'Oh, that's cool. You take pictures?'

'Yeah. Got a camera. SLR.'

'Nice. I've just got this shitty little thing.' It's so awkward trying to look through all the stuff in my bag with my gloves on. Can't figure out what is what when I can't feel it. This must be it. Yup. Lifting the small silver £30 affair for Matt to see; it's worked to divert his attention from the sky and to bring his eyes to me. Look at me.

But he's looking at the camera, and he scoffs, 'Heh. How many mega pixels?'

'Five.' The offending gadget is dropped back with my wallet, my keys, emergency make-up. I'm really not apologetic about how crap my camera is. Not sure how much I care. It's there to take pictures of other people, never me. I know what other people look like, so as long as I have some kind of memoir of an occasion, it doesn't have to be la-dee-da hi-tech.

Why is he smiling? Oh my God, I can feel myself blushing. I'm embarrassed by his *smile*. What did I expect? In all honesty, a smirk at best. Or maybe he'd roll his eyes and not say a word. But he's actually smiling.

'It's hardly the best thing on the market, kid, but it does the job.'

Kid. What is 'kid'? Whatever, it sounds nice when he says it.

'Where are you from?'

'Edinburgh.' His attention is back to the Meadows, eyes watching the path that we're walking down before they flicker to the play-park just in the distance. It's like magic, the way his expression completely changes, the way he turns back to me with *that* smile. 'Let's go to the park.' There's something slightly dangerous about his words too, like he's announcing a pirate adventure.

There's no need to reply because I'm already following him, almost chasing him across the grass. It's dry, thank

God, but there's still the threat of dog poo. Under the influence of beer, and with the backs of my pumps slipping off my heels, I'm not running as fast as I should to keep up. Still, I'm going too fast and everything is moving.

'Hurry up then!' His voice is calling from just ahead of me, through the blue gates. Steady, steady; must stand still so that everything can focus. High, low, high, low; Matt is rattling the frames supporting the swing he's on.

The swing beside his is tangled. Some Buckie-drinking dickheads have wound it round the top bar. So I take the next seat along. It's probably safer this way anyway, dizzying enough just to watch Matt swing his legs out, then in, out, then in. It's nicer just rocking backwards and forwards, scuffing the soles of my shoes across the rubber beneath me.

'What do you do on your days off?' His voice is close and then far, half lost between the swooshing of the chains in the wind. 'Apart from going to really bad student parties.'

'Not a lot.' Suddenly I'm swinging a little bit harder, putting in a little more effort like it's going to save me from my status as 'boring.' 'I like...films.'

He's slowed down now, both of us swinging at the same time. But I'm back, and he's forward, 'What? Every film ever? Or just some kinds of films?'

Oh ha ha.

'Well... I like world cinema. Especially French and Asian films.' It's pretty much impossible to say that without sounding like a pretentious wanker. I can feel myself cringing under the weight of my own interests; why can't I just like *Sex and the City* and *Shrek* like everyone else?

'Seen *Battle Royale*?'

Of course I've seen *Battle Royale*. Only the seminal work of Japanese cinema. Maybe he's just testing me, making sure I'm not thick. Either way, it's a connection, something to link us together. My interest is definitely piqued. 'Yeah. I *love* that film.'

'Me too. The second one was fucking stupid.' My agreement is silent as he slows down just to sit, his own feet kicking at some stones. He's wearing a ruined pair of Converse, scribbled on with permanent marker and biro. 'So French films? Shit like *Amelie*, right?'

Or maybe he wasn't testing me. Maybe they're the only non-Hollywood films that he knows. 'Yup, exactly. Stuff like *Amelie*.' Urgh, who's that now? My hands are digging through my bag and I'm having the same problem, trying to guess phone from camera or...

'Hello? Lisa? Are you okay? What?' Why is she freaking out so much? For God's - 'No, I'm not at home. Yeah. Matt.' The party has made her drunk and deaf, '*Matt*. I dunno. Right. I'll be there in a minute, okay?'

'Drunken friend?' Matt could probably hear her screeching from where he was sitting, through the phone and the air between us.

'Yeah, it's Lisa. She's at the party and wants to go home but she doesn't want to walk by herself.'

'Sure...like there aren't enough guys there that want to take her home.'

Suddenly I'm far too tired to care enough to defend Lisa, but I make a frown and shake my head a little.

'Oh, there will be. Just she doesn't want to go back with them. They seemed kinda creepy.'

'Fair point.' Matt's shuffling off the swing, moving towards the gate. 'Alright, let's get you back to the house of fun.'

We're walking back together, retracing our footsteps to the party. Adjusting my scarf, pulling at the hem of my skirt, checking the mud on my shoes, dragging fingers through my hair. When I drop my hand, my breathing slows, and I concentrate on how close it is to his, that we're nearly touching fingers. Barely, just barely, our pinkies brush.

I want to be remembered. I want him to think of the party, and think of the girl he went to the park with, to remember what she looked like, how she adjusted her coat, how the colour of her nails matched the colour of her scarf. I'm frightened, almost, to smile, in case it doesn't look right. Even if later he's too busy in his life for me, it's important that I'm noticed, that being like this right now looks to him like a still in his photo album.

FIVE

Sarah

'Sarah! Say-rah!'

Yup, was right the first time round; it *is* Naomi's voice calling through the bedroom door, over the voices on the television, through the wardrobe door. I'm practically standing in the thing, digging out horrendous and long-forgotten clothes. 'You can come in, Naomi.'

Standing awkwardly in the doorway, she hovers, eyes flicking to Johnny Depp on the screen, 'Uhm... it's your mum on the phone.'

The offending piece of clothing is thrown to floor, 'Mum?' That doesn't make sense. Why didn't she call my mobile? Following Naomi out into the corridor, to the kitchen, checking my phone to make sure there's no missed call. 'Hello?'

'Hello, darling, how are you?'

Since when was "darling" in vogue? Is she *crying*? Mum, are you okay?'

'Oh, Sarah.' Uh oh. That tone in her voice is desperate.

'Mum, are you okay? Has something happened?' Oh my God, the dog is dead. Or Granddad's dead, or Grandma's cancer's come back.

Her breath rattles against the speaker, shaky in my ear, 'It's your father...' What? *What?* '... your father and I have... decided to get a divorce.'

'What?' Heard her, but there's no way this is serious. Mum's not the type to joke but this is just stupid. 'Mum... it was probably just an argument...' Though God only knows what might have happened this time.

'No, darling, Sarah, it's true. We decided -' Her voice breaks off and I can almost feel the heaving of her sobs on the other end of the line. There was no 'we' involved in this decision.

'So... where are you? What happened? Are you at the house?' No need to ask after Dad. The idiot can take care of himself; he always does, while Mum got into a mess.

'I'm staying with your grandfather just now, until things get sorted out.'

'What happened?' Please don't say that Dad got with someone else.

'Oh, well... we both knew it would happen, dear. It's been going to happen for years. I -' In her pausing is the sound of a lipstick being opened. I swear that's what it is. She's not pulling herself together; she's drawing a smile on her lips. 'It was just a matter of time. It would have happened years ago but...'

What the fuck? She's not even paying attention to what she's saying. She'll be sitting at the dressing table in the spare room, playing with the marbled comb set. 'But what?' Really, I don't have time for this. Got a wardrobe to sort and I'm missing *Sleepy Hollow*.

'It just wouldn't have been fair, Sarah, to you.'

'Sorry?'

'Well, if your father and I had divorced that first time it wouldn't have been fair. You were in the middle of your exams and it wouldn't have been fair to move you to a different school. And you know how important that school was, how brilliant it was for art and design, and for you, the people I had to talk to get you a place.'

What the fuck? 'Oh, so you're saying it's my fault that you and Dad were so unhappy for years. When exactly was 'that first time'?'

'Oh...it was a long time ago now. But Sarah, it's not important. The year doesn't matter.' She's panicking now. What did she expect? Oh, I'm so sorry, Mum. That's terrible, Mum. Let me put my life on hold for you, Mum.

'Well, at least you're happy now, hmm? You and Dad, away from me, away from each other.'

'Sarah...' She knows I'm pissed off but she just can't figure out what to do about it. No doubt she's busy checking her wrinkles in the mirror.

'Okay. Well, thanks for letting me know.' Staring at the cradle, eyes blurring the button out of focus. Hang up? Her voice is wailing at the other end and it's the start of a horrible headache. The receiver makes a clatter as it drops; it doesn't rest in its box, but it lunges to the kitchen tiles, bouncing on the coils.

'Sarah, are you okay?'

God, just so fed up of people saying my name. Didn't mean to make such a scene with the phone, so I'm picking it up, slowly. Nothing has happened. But Naomi's closing in behind me. 'Yeah, just dropped the phone.' Oops, silly me.

'Alright.' She needs to get past, so I move. If I didn't, there's no way she'd fit through the gap between the counters. Naomi insists she's on a diet, but I've seen the snacks in the cupboard, and the empty pizza box in the bin. I don't mean to be mean, but diets totally don't work that way.

'Could you please bring out my bottle of wine?' Since she's rummaging through the fridge anyway.

'The pinot grigio?'

'Yep. Want a glass?'

She almost looks frightened by the offer and shakes her head softly, grabbing her nachos and dip, 'Want some of this? Just going to put a film on.'

Eww, sour cream and chive. 'What you watching?'

'*Clueless*. Got it in the sale today.'

Sometimes I'm secretly glad of her penchant for old-school chick flicks. 'Alright. I haven't seen that film in ye-ears.'

Trailing out of the kitchen and through the hall, into the living room, dumping down on our respective sofas to watch the film. What is wrong with this wine? It smells okay, I think, but it tastes sour.

Once upon a time those garish nineties outfits were so cool; there was nothing better than a midriff and badly fitting jeans. My fingers prod at my own stomach, self-conscious and apprehensive poking. I never was Alicia, all skinny and blonde and bubbly and ridiculous in a cute way. I was more like Brittany, only I never got round to sorting myself out. Once a mess, always a mess.

'Nachos?'

Staring into the open end of the bag, the cheesy smell is awful and overwhelming. I'm trying hard not to scrunch up my nose, as it would be rude to make my disgust too obvious. 'No thanks.' I'm hungry for chocolate. 'Gonna find something else to eat.'

Getting up off the sofa is such an effort; swinging my legs back round, feet on the floor, putting down my glass to push myself to stand. Fuck it, this bottle's coming with me. What do I have to eat? Please, let there be chocolate, of any kind. It's freezing out. There's no way I'm crossing the street. Not looking like this. Too lazy to make face and

dress properly. Fuck it, I'm *not* too lazy, I'm just depressed. Chocolate pudding. When did I even buy this? Turning it over, good, it's not out of date. Microwave, come here. Just two minutes. Plate, fork. Turn it over, carefully... There! One hot, steaming chocolate pudding. Take it to settle on my bed, surrounded by pillows and ugly plush toys. Got to blow on it first. My mouth is full of the taste of soft chocolate, thickening in my throat as the tears start to fall. My nose, my mouth, all my breathing is suddenly restricted and the pudding is stuck at the back on my throat. Swallow, swallow. Need to swallow or I'll choke. Everything is dripping and I feel like I'm melting, my vision fuzzy as I stare at the offending food on the plate. Help...
Brr Brr. Brr Brr.

Matt

'Hello, Scottish Power.'

'Matt?'

'Ya, it's me.'

'Are you busy?'

A copy of *FHM* is lying open by his knee on the bed and the screen is paused, control pad resting idly in his free hand; it's impossible to play on veteran mode *and* talk on the phone. 'Not so much. What you up to?'

'I'm...eating a tinned chocolate pudding.'

'Ni-ice. What kind? Cadbury's or Tesco value?'

'I-it's Tesco b-but not value.'

'That's not so bad.'

What is she even saying? Matt can't quite make out the words. Her voice is thick with something other than just chocolate. The sound in the ear piece is muffled with what he can only guess is a sigh.

'Sarah, are you okay...?' Matt surprises himself with his own tenderness; didn't even know his voice could sound like that. Is she *crying?* In a confused pause, he just looks at his phone, hearing an unmistakable sob even at this small distance. 'Sarah,' and he wonders why it always seems so necessary to repeat someone's name when trying to be comforting, 'What happened?'

The next noise she makes is pretty rank, but at least she apologises, 'Sorry. I'm sorry. I shouldn't have called. I'm just. It's just. I'm...'

None of this is making any sense, 'It's okay, just take your time. What's going on?'

'It's Mum. And Dad. They've...broken up. I mean, divorced. They're getting a fucking divorce.'

This is way out of his territory. Sure, anyone knows what to say if someone's died. Everyone knows the right words to use in case of disappointment. But divorce just brings up too much; relationships, childhood, and actually that's pretty much everything. 'Oh.' So his guess is that this is bad. That she's not taken the news well. But is she team Mum or team Dad? Matt's silence is awkward but it gives her space to vent.

'It's just so...irresponsible and just...inconvenient.' She sounds about as eloquent as he is, swallowing hard as she makes her way through her pudding regardless. 'But it's like she doesn't care. Like she enjoys the drama. She doesn't give a shit how I feel and thinks it's all just a bit of fun. Dad's been treating her like shit for years and now he's fucked off, probably with some junkie boy or girl. And all Mum will care about is the money and where it goes and they think they can do what they want.'

'Well...they kind of can.' Shit. That was definitely the wrong thing to say, but it's true.

'What?'

'Well, sounds like they need to go their separate ways. I mean, yeah, they're your parents but they have their own lives to think about too.'

'But what about me?'

What about her? He doesn't even really know her. 'Okay, so...what was your relationship with your parents like?'

'Horrible. It was like they compensated for being so shit by buying me stuff.' Her laugh is scornful on the other end, and she coughs, almost choking. 'Stuff I didn't even want. Then at some point Dad thought it would be fun to spend less and less time around the house. He never tried to hide his affairs, so Mum didn't even try to hide her drinking or her ridiculous spending sprees. They always tried to seem so proper, with their stiff upper lips and their boring jobs, but they're just a couple of teenagers.'

At last, she takes a breath. That was some rant. 'But you're your own person. You don't have to deal with that shit anymore.'

The start of her sentence comes out as a series of noises, 'I know. It's just... Mum said she's been unhappy with Dad for years so I don't get why they just sat around, pretending to play happy families.'

'Maybe because they had you to think about?' This pause is too long. Has he said the wrong thing? Maybe she hung up. 'Hello?'

She breathes and he waits, running his thumb over the buttons on the control pad. 'I guess...maybe.' Finally, it talks. 'Maybe I'm just being selfish but it's just one more kick in the teeth.'

'But why are you letting them? Look, if they were bullies from your high school years or whatever, would you let them bother you now? Would you give a shit what they did?'

'No... But -'

'So why let them upset you so much? Yeah, okay, so they're your parents but it doesn't sound like they did a great job of it.' No offence. Oops.

'But it's just... I mean, you're right. If they were anyone else in the world I would hate them but they're my parents so I don't, ya know?'

Actually, he doesn't. 'Hmm...' Non-committal noises.

'I really don't need this right now. At least if they're going to divorce I don't need Mum on the phone trying to gain sympathy votes.'

'Listen, like I said, they're doing their thing and you're doing yours. It hurts because they're your parents and you love them,' is that what she was getting at? 'But you're better than that.'

'Thanks.' Small and soft; there's a hint of a smile in that voice.

'No problem. What I'm here for.' This stuff is seriously tiring. Holding the phone tighter to his ear, *FHM* is pushed carefully onto the floor before he rolls onto his back on the bed. The ceiling is disgusting.

'Sorry for phoning.' And she gasps like something has happened, but then so does he, the control pad falling to the floor. The game resumes, and it's really loud. Shit. Need to pause it. Fuck, falls out of bed.

'Sorry about that. Just dropped something.'

She laughs, but almost like she doesn't want to, given the state she's in, 'Me too. Dropped the plate and got chocolate sauce everywhere.'

'Ha! Well I got shot.'

'What?'

'I got shot. Multiple rounds.'

'What?' She's really not getting it.

'Call of Duty.' A pause while she racks her brains, 'Uh...Playstation?' Maybe she doesn't know what that is either?

'Oh... right. Yeah. Sorry.'

'What for?'

'For your loss.'

See? Consoling death is definitely easier. 'It's okay. I'll just have to reload my game and...' Playing along, a voice full of woe, 'I'm sure I can carry on. It'll be okay. It won't be easy, but it'll be okay.'

'There, there.'

Laughter sounds good across telephone waves. Crackly in an old Nokia earpiece. Laughter is definitely an improvement on sighs and choked silence. 'Better?'

'Mhm, much.'

'Good. I'm a doctor, you know. Laughter is the best medicine.'

'Uh huh, I'm sure. It's a shame you can't see me rolling my eyes at you.'

Actually, that is a shame. 'We need to remedy that. I need to hang out with your rolling eyes sometime. Doctors orders and all that.'

'Really? Well, if it's doctors orders then I guess I can't really object.'

'You couldn't resist anyway. Even if I wasn't a doctor.'

'Not so sure about that one. My powers of resistance are pretty good.'

'Sounds like a challenge. We'll see.' She's funny. Despite awkward rants, this girl seems to actually have something to say for herself. Makes a change. 'Alright, this doctor is out. You need to have yourself a nice bath, a hot chocolate then a good long sleep, okay?'

'Okay.'

Wow, that was easy enough. Good effort. Good work. 'Good. And if you need to call me up again, feel free.'

'Don't worry, I will. But hopefully next time my chat will have improved.'

Haha! Laughing out loud again, this is healthy, 'I hope so.'

SIX

Sarah

Why did Lisa even phone last night? Why does she always have to do that? Personally, I was happier on my bedroom floor with the sour pinot grigio. It'll be fun, she said. You've been working too hard. You need to let your hair down. Her voice is so whiney but she always makes everything seem so tempting. It really did sound like it was going to be fun. But it wasn't at the time and it's even less so now.

Staring. Just staring at the computer screen, waiting for the orders to sort themselves out. If I look at the spreadsheets any longer my eyes will fall out of my head, or they'll melt all down my face. My face, is a mess. Avoiding all mirrors is one hundred percent necessary this morning. Tinted moisturiser, concealer, liquid, mousse, powder foundations, and still the bags under my eyes show. I need rest. Real doctor or not, Matt was right. I needed a bath and a rest but here I am, hung over and I'm sure pretty smelly too. Least it's just me and Laura today and Laura's incense covers all traces of vodka and any hint of sour wine.

'Sarah?' Oh my God, could she shout any louder? I'm really not that far away. 'Sarah? Can I have some help in here, please?'

So much effort just getting up from the chair. It's warm in here, cosy with the heater at my feet. There are no windows in my little office so I can just cosy up and keep quiet and warm, do my work at a snail's leisurely pace. Stood up way too quickly, the light's too bright, everything so sore. Yes, Lisa, a swing band does sound like good fun. Dancing like a maniac all night and spraining my ankle? Even better. Standing just on the edge of the shop floor, everything feels like it's swimming and suddenly I'm regretting the decision of a kebab on the way home.

'Thank you, dear. Do you mind serving these customers while I talk to this couple about wedding flowers?' She looks positively excited. One, weddings are a huge cause of happy celebration but two, they're her biggest earner. The more weddings, the merrier. For both of us.

'Of course.' Trying my hardest to shine and seem pleasant, but I'm sure my forehead is too oily this morning and my steps towards the cash register are hardly energetic. 'Hi there.' Lesson number one, treat the customer with friendliness and respect. Okay, I can do this. The smile is happening somehow but I'm not really looking at them. Just scan the stuff through, smile and nod at the right time, give the right amount of laughter and ring through the sale. It's not as easy as it sounds. Not today. Please, stop the boring chitchat, my face hurts. That, and I'm worried about throwing up inside the cash drawer. The smell of the coins is overwhelming. Just keep hold of the desk, don't fall over. Stand straight; work with me, feet.

Huh? There's Matt. At least, I think it's Matt. I want to wave, want to run outside and wave. I want him to come by and notice me. But he doesn't know I work here. Pretty sure he doesn't. Damn, should have told him. Right now, it doesn't look like he's noticing anything. Can't even see his face, his shoulders hunched up like that and his eyes trained on the ground. Maybe it's not even him. But if it is him, where is he going? What is he thinking? Maybe about a girl he knows whose parents are getting divorced, maybe about a phone call and a promise to meet soon. Matt, what are you thinking?

SEVEN

Matt

Fuck. Fucking *fuck*. Just walking. Walking, going nowhere, going anywhere. Getting away. Spiders are shit at the best of times, but especially when they're that size and turning green to red to green to red. It's not real, Matt, it's not real. But there's this battle, always a battle. What's real? What isn't? Fucked if he knows anymore. Giant spiders don't just appear on TV sets and they seriously don't change colour. Hell, even a chameleon does't change like that. Shit. So over this - he's been through this before. It's all in his head, all in his head and he knows it. So what's with the running?

Fucking hell, it's hot. He really needs to stop before he passes out. People are walking, talking, carrying bags, carrying babies, laughing, running. Why are they running? Perched on a wall, Matt's not part of the crowd anymore. Just sitting there, minding his own business. Further down the wall some hobo is picking old chewing gum off the bricks. Matt can smell him from where he's sitting and it's making him nauseous - that horrendous stench of rotten everything, piss and stale alcohol. Oh God. On an empty stomach. All you can throw up is bile, boy. No harm done.

So much for a refreshing rest. Shuffle, instead of walk; that's the best he can do.

Pharmacy. Should he go in? Yes, or no? Yes. And then? And he complains, makes a scene, gets laughed at, gets thrown another doctor's number, gets printed another prescription. Back at square one. Why repeat what didn't work before? Just take them, the doctor said, and the course will work itself out. You've got to stick with it, he said, stick with it and you'll notice the difference - feel better in no time.

No time does not translate into three weeks. So the answer is no. No pharmacy.

The pub is dead, but so it would be at this time in the morning. Offer as much tea and coffee and 'freshly baked homemade' scones as you like but no cunt's heading to a pub for their breakfast. But Chris, Mr. Manager, in all his infinite wisdom knows best. Stupid bastard.

'Matt. It's a bit early for you, isn't it?' Oh haha, you're so fucking funny with your little chuckle, sputtering away with your shitty sarcasm. Looking at your watch, looking at the bar clock, looking at your watch.

'Oh ha ha, yeah Chris! Oh my God, you're right! I'm kinda early for work. Could have had a lie-in.'

'What are you doing here?'

What the fuck? 'Came to ask about shifts.'

'You know about holidays: no.'

Dick. 'I want to do the late night ones. Give the day shifts to Dan.'

'You talked to Dan about this?'

Well, duh. 'Yes, and he said he'd like to do the day shifts, and I'll take the night shifts.'

'Look, I don't really care who's here as long as there's *someone* behind the bar. Sort it.' His voice is low, and his breath smells like a dirty hamster cage. So good of him to keep polite when there's one customer on one of the sofas. Excellent customer service. Excellent.

'That's great. Thanks so much.' Matt's mouth hurts with the pain of pretending to be pleased. Actually, he *is* pleased - this'll help sort out the insomnia. At least he'll have something to do and somewhere to be during the night. Which means not seeing Chris' crater-pocked face every day. Haha, yes. Extra bonus.

'Glad to be of service, Matt. Just make sure you clear up and lock up properly, okay? I would actually like to come back to my pub in the morning.'

'Can do!' Matt doesn't even consider gracing Chris with a wave goodbye. This is it, Chris; he's pretty much out of your life and it's your loss. Not that you'll notice the absence.

But how can *he* get out of his own life? God, he's so fucking fed up of feeling like a moany bastard and thinking like a complete dick.

Stuck at the traffic lights, watching taxis and buses zoom past. An ambulance sounds in the background, somewhere. Still too far away to tell if it's coming towards him or away. Come at him; jump in front of it; smiling like an idiot, feet soaked by dirty puddle water. Weirdly, it's only now that he notices the stench of the stuff; how many drains are blocked in this street, in this whole fucking city? Nee naw, nee naw. Is the ambulance speeding to an emergency call, or is it speeding with a dying man in the back? Just another suicide, wasting NHS time, taking up a table and bleeding on a floor. It's inconsiderate. What would happen if he *did* jump in front? The paramedics would be pissed off; his life getting in the way of another much more worthwhile. If Matt was attending, he knows he probably wouldn't even try to help. Oh, his brains are all over the road. Fuck this, let's get this poor old lady to the hospital. Shit, he's still breathing, but we've got a pregnant woman to take care of. Two heads are better than one.

Crossing the road anyway, but fuck he wishes he hadn't. Just down the street a group of school kids. There's no way they're even in high school yet. Just a bunch of boys, probably laughing about a Star Wars joke. This one has all his puppy fat, but maybe one day he'll lose it and be the talk of the school. In the meantime he's munching some Space Raiders, his friends all chewing on Irn Bru bars and Snickers. Snickers, because they have nuts and make you a man. It's cool to eat peanuts. They're not even allowed in school. When was the last time he ate some chocolate and it wasn't complicated with something else? Like a girl, or depression, or a bad family holiday.

Not the fucking Royal Mile. Casio watch bleeps 13.06. So why are there so many people around? Surely some of them must have jobs. There can't honestly be this many unemployed people in Edinburgh. Lunch time, maybe. But they're walking so leisurely, stopping to look at the least insignificant things. So they're a bunch of tourists, browner than the rest of us, chattering in a language too fast to make out, not that he could understand anyway. Why take a photo there? Get a better angle of Calton Hill from further down the bridge. That hotel is seriously not worth leaning over for. Get yourself hurt for nothing. Still, Matt takes a peek, though he's looking for something different. Over the edge. The ledge is currently empty, but it's too wet to be much fun. This spitting rain is just too slippery to make the moment last. Only two days ago and the bridge was closed, police tape cordoning off either end. Making people walk through Cockburn St to get anywhere. Seriously, the guy was fucked out of his mind, so no wonder. Men with megaphones, coaxing, shouting. At Waverley station every cunt had his camera out, snapping the progress, lenses ready for the jump, or an accidental slip. Matt can't believe he didn't have his camera. In negative, black and white, soft focus lens. That shit would be magic.

Congratulations, Matt, you have missed out on another wonderful opportunity to succeed at life. Prize? Sorry, no prize. Not even a cheap keyring, a little fob with "Matt Fails" in a neat red logo.

What the fuck is he doing on Princes Street? All these materialist machines running from one end to the other. The shops are all the same. Several Topshops, a few H&Ms, multiple HMVs. It doesn't ever seem particularly necessary. But somehow it is, and somehow it works, and somehow Matt finds himself dodging charity beggars in luminous coats. Save the Children? No thanks. Endangered Chimpanzees? How is that even a charity?

'Hi there, interested in helping sufferers of mental illness?'

Oh really?

'Uhm... sure, why not?' She looks shocked that she's managed to flag someone down, frizzy curls stuck to her forehead with rain. Green Doc Martins; not a good look. He's about to be interrogated by a self-righteous lesbian. Bet she self-harmed in school because no one understood her.

'Well...we're basically a charity set up to help individuals and families to cope with mental illness. And -'

She could be talking about anything right now; his main concern is that she missed a bit when she waxed her moustache: swear she'd win in a beard growing contest.

Huh. Wow, Matt checks his week's stubble; actually pretty impressive, nice around the jaw. Shit, she's asking him a question.

'Sorry?'

'Do you have a debit or credit card?'

'Yeah, okay.' This just isn't even funny anymore. 'Thanks, bye.'

Battling his way back home, feeling like Richard Ashcroft in that Verve video. Walking in the wrong direction, as per, moving away from tourist spots, Kodak moments, herds of foreign kids. Twenty minutes away, there's so much comfort on his quiet street; no one needs to be there. An optional place, en route to far more important things.

'Hey Matt!' Giggling as their voices come in unison from the living room.

Is she really still here? He likes her but - 'Alright, folks?' Standing like an awkward third wheel in the doorway. Sue's reclining on the sofa, head attached to Dan's thigh.

'Chris alright about the shifts?' His heard turns with vague half-interest, eyes flicking back to the television screen. They all pause to watch some ugly rat dog being dragged into a vet surgery.

'Yeah, was fine.'

Dan runs a hand over his freshly shaved baldness, probably still looking for his hair. Told him it was a bad idea, but Sue has ruling vote. Whipped. 'Gonna put a film on or something?'

That's not even a question that makes sense, but Matt shakes his head anyway, reaching to take his jacket off. 'Nah. Maybe. In a bit.' Disappears into his room before Sue's eyes piss him off any more. Bitch might as well live there. Maybe if she did she wouldn't think it was so necessary to lie around in her pyjamas. Dan might enjoy the 'contours' of her body but spare him, Lord spare him, from those nipples. So hard to work with two people that you heard having sex all night, especially when you have to see the dirty face the next day, eyeliner drunkenly smudged.

The box has to be somewhere. Matt, stop your fucking moaning. Really not needed. Where the fuck is it? Probably decided last time to hide it as far back as possible. Stretched out, hand reaching past God knows what; shoes, lost socks, old magazines. What the - a pizza crust? Shit, it's almost green. There. His fingertips brush against something cold and metal. Reach just a little further and he's got it. Sitting in the midst of bedroom debris, Matt crosses his legs, placing the little lunch box at his feet.

Does he really want to do this? Stupid, stupid idea. Long behind him. Supposed to be cutting this out. Don't do it. But why not? His body, his rules. People drink, people take drugs, people go snowboarding. Matt does this. Everyone needs their endorphins, and right now Matt really needs his. Before it goes wrong. Take it in small doses, do it while he's level headed, ahead of the game. Fingers running over the embossed Batman logos. Fingers moving to the small metal catches. Undoing them. Hand pushing the lid open, eyes staring at the contents.

Nail scissors.
Letter opener.
Vegetable knife.
Assortment of razor blades.
Tweezers.

Fingers clasping round the nail scissors this time. They know what they're doing. Open, close. Open, close. Fingers keep hold through the small hoops while his jumper is removed and the short sleeves of his t-shirt pushed back. Don't look now. Don't ruin this for yourself. Not again.

Inhale.

Choked with the sweet scent of weed, drifting in beneath the door. Canned barking from the TV.

Exhale.
Slower. Take your time.

Fuck this.

Eyes closed, breathing softly through the relief.

Metal snags at skin.

Start again.

Cleaner cut.

Shit.

The scissors drag through a recent scab, picking red crust, bleeding starting fresh.

Nail scissors lying closed in the palm of his hand, blood hot as it oozes over scabs and skin.

Can't take this.

Can't take this.

It's all in his head, all in his head. But there's no point. Everything is fuzzy: empty fuzziness. Head bangs against the wardrobe, stinging eyes. Stinging eyes, stinging arm.

So much better.

Hand punches the floor, carpet burn cutting into his knuckles and fingers. Why go through this? Always the same. He's under control.

Help.

EIGHT

Sarah

All these women with their tiny little bodies in their tiny little clothes. Looking so incredible. Flat stomach, skinny arms, no thighs; the envy of every girl and the desire of every boy. Okay, so I'm about a stone and a half heavier than I used to be. But once I was one of these girls. Ribs on show, dangly limbs, disappearing waist.

So what's it all about? Pain for fashion, a cry out for attention, whatever you want to call it. My anorexia is my deal. Do it because I want to. It's got nothing to do with celebrities in Vogue, it's got nothing to do with a need for control. This is my decision. Male attention? Yeah, right. A man will fuck anyone or anything he can get his hands on, even the 'sensitive types'. Too fat or too thin, a guy will find something he's attracted to between two legs. It's much harder, on the other hand, to gain the appreciation of women. Want a girl to notice you and you have to try harder. In no way is this a sexual thing; that's definitely not what I'm after. But to be the centre of attention, to walk into a crowded room and have every head turn to catch another look at you. People want to be you, they're so jealous. Envy my dress, envy my hair colour, envy my shoes, envy my purse; go ahead. Go out and collect the outfit, try as hard as you can. My bone structure? That's something you can't have. Not the way my face is thin, my cheekbones flushed and pink. Not the way my clavicles sit pronounced above a strapless top. Not the way my hips protrude, sturdy and inviting, the furthest thing from a squashy muffin top. Seven stone and the world is at my feet; everyone wants to know me, even if it's just to try and make me feel better, giving them some purpose when they tell you how skinny and pale I look. When you're skinny, you're attractive to everyone. Whatever the reason.

It's not easy. A body takes hard work and a lot of effort, especially if you like food. It's a love-hate thing. But it's not like you don't have to eat at all: a cheeseburger a day keeps the weight at bay. Looking for thinspiration? Yes, I am. Click.

More women and girls, posting their calorie intake, posting pictures of their ankle fat. Complaining that the family made her sit down to a meal and she felt forced to eat three times her usual intake. Talking about ways to keep sugar levels up when she exercises too much in one day. Considering bulimia as an alternative. If you need to purge, spin round really fast after drinking loads of diet Coke. And make sure not to get finger marks on your hand or people will find out. Don't eat spicy foods because they'll hurt on the way up. But everyone knows that being sick is just stupid, because the acid from the vomit ruins teeth enamel. What use is there in being skinny if you can't even crack a smile?

This website has a huge advertisement on the side. Not free spa samples, not donations to keep pro-ana sites running, but big and bold and green: suicide prevention. Okay, so that's great. Pictures of girls I would kill to look like, hips that I would murder to show, then suicide prevention. These bodies are incredible. At least, not many make me want to die. Pretty bodies, all dressed up beside a big green suicide prevention ad. Last time I checked, suicide had nothing to do with losing weight. Why do that? Why spend all that time, endure all those stomach cramps, for nothing? Appreciate your body lying in a coffin? No point.

These girls blogging about how great their parents are for not noticing. Mum always thought anorexia was great fun: 'You look fantastic, dear. Like something cut right out of Vogue.' Probably the best compliment Mum ever gave me, and really she'd never been more proud. At eight stone and with a degree, all she can say is, 'That's really nice.' Yes Mum, it is 'really nice', really nice to get a history degree, really nice to have four years of sweat, blood and tears. Really nice.

I need to be sick. Not a throaty nausea, but something twisting in the pit of my stomach. These next pictures can't even be called sexy. These women would be better off in a copy of Gray's *Anatomy*. Any skinnier and I would see the outline of her lungs and kidneys.

Omg she is so cute I wish I cud luk like that. Yeh, she is my thinspiration. Evry day I luk at her.

This is probably the best punctuation and spelling I've seen on the whole site. Even the 'admin' can't type to save themselves. Somehow it demeans everything this site has been selling me. It's not about self-betterment. It's suddenly not about dealing with disorders anymore. It's all a fad, just a game for teenagers. You hit twenty, and all of a sudden it's not cool to be anorexic anymore. So I'm too old for this game now. Anorexia is getting bad press: think skinny Twiglet, think idiot blonde.

What the fuck am I doing here? Skeleton isn't pretty. Nearly, but not quite. This sick feeling isn't disgust. Perhaps it could be, but really I know it's guilt. I'll admit that even now. Guilt at going back to what I promised myself I'd given up. Like Mum cares, like anybody cares. But if anyone's going to care it has to be me.

I press the red x at the top right hand corner, and the page is gone. My hands grab at my waist; how much fat is in that fistful? Fingers pinching at my cheeks. Flexing my ankle, trying to find a way to rest my leg that makes my calves look smaller. Knee bent, toes pointing upwards. Willing the fat to vanish. If I could take a knife, cut around the flesh of my belly. If I could pull it all out, throw it away.

No one would need to know.

Even if I lose all this weight again, I'll still want more gone. It's not enough until I disappear.

NINE

His forearms are crossed with white lines. Criss cross, criss cross. Like a game of noughts and crosses where the players gave up halfway through. Grids of stretched skin, puckered and healed. My fingertips move lightly over the scars, barely grazing the bumps. Does a scar still hurt, even after it's healed and turned silver? These were no accident. Not the bites of a dog, or accidental scratches. They're too pretty, too organised, too deliberate to be the work of cat's claws. His arm flexes, pulling away as my fingers curl around his wrist. Twisting behind me, his cough is uncomfortable and my back becomes cold as he moves away.

'I'm sorry.'
All that I can manage, even though I want to know. I know how they happened, but I want to know why.

'Nah. It's okay.'

'They're old, though.' Confident and assuring, because I know.

'Yeah... they are.'

Matt, please don't feel awkward. 'I have some. Just like that.' Sitting curled in front of him my head nods toward my thigh where beneath my jeans are two small scars, where I had tried it once but couldn't carry on.

His arms reach around my shoulders, cuddling close as he pulls up the sleeve of his jacket again. 'That one there, that was a dog. Rottweiler. She was a little excited and jumped up. Wound up with a burst lip too.' Wrapped inside his arms I can feel his chest moving with his laughter, 'Still alive so far as I know, even though they wanted to put her down.'

It's silent for a while. Some traffic moves along the road, a few late night taxis. We're hidden from view, boxed in a children's play frame in the park. The same park. Just sitting and staring, too tired for swings.

'I'm sorry I called you out so late.'

'Don't worry about it. I was up anyway.'

His body shifts, face looming round to look at mine, 'At 2am? Doing what?'

'Just... y'know, looking at stuff online. Pissing around on YouTube.' And trawling through pro-ana sites. Could I tell him?

'God, I could spend my whole day that way.'

Everyone hates awkward silence; the few seconds where no one says anything but the air is thick with intention, be it something you want to say or something you're waiting to hear.

'I'm glad you came. It's just nice to have someone to talk to sometimes.' His words are strained and slow, like he's not used to talking things out.

'Don't you have any flatmates or anything?' It's not that I mind. It's good for me to be away from the computer screen, calming to look out across the dully lit park, watching an empty expanse of green and sky.

'He's busy. With his girlfriend.'

Seems strange, both of us looking out in the same direction, not being able to see his face. 'Aww... you jealous?'

'Of her? Definitely. Thought he'd pick me over any girl.' His laugh is natural, like he's used to this, like there's some kind of running joke between him and his flatmate. Then the silence lapses again and desperately I need to think of something, anything to say, and I'm edging very close to talking about some stupid YouTube video.

'I had to get out of there. I had to get out of the flat, before I did something stupid.'

'What do you mean?' Trying not to sound nosy, because I already know. Just, I want to hear him say it; I want to be let in.

'Hurt myself.' He pronounces each word clearly, so there's no mistaking what he had said, there's no need to ask again. I can hear him breathe a shaky sigh of relief, but his body immediately freezes, rigid. Don't be scared, Matt.

I just want to jump inside his brain, inside that mind. What's going on in here?

'Look, Matt, you know you can call me whenever, right? Even if it's just to clear your mind. And I'm pretty much a night owl so I don't mind meeting up like this, if you like.'

Turning and reaching, but he's disappeared from behind me. He's crawled to the other side of the platform, swinging his legs before jumping.

'Is there anything you want to talk about?'

Matt

Nah, Matt's done. That's as much talking as she'll get out of him.

'Talk about what?'

Along the monkey bars it takes a lot of effort to keep his knees raised high. His feet keep sinking to the ground, but to let them touch would make it just too easy.

'Well...about anything.' She looks embarrassed as she tries to find a way down. She could take the wet slide or climb down the rope. Assessing both, it takes a moment before she opts for the rope, though she might as well have just jumped, risked the tumble.

'You okay?' Matt catches himself laughing. She's obviously alright, brushing wood chippings and God knows what from her tights, but it's polite to ask.

It's a welcome distraction from the topic at hand. Hands, his, the palms hurt from rubbing against the rusty metal bars. Sarah just seemed like the obvious choice. At least, she was willing. The pretext of a romantic evening in the park is always good. He wasn't lying when he said he needed to talk. Really, he did. But what should he say? 'Hi, you don't know me but I self-harm and I needed to get out the house before I did it again. Yes, again. I cut myself today. Hmm? Yes, that's right, with nail scissors.'

But then, she tried to get too deep. No, she didn't. She was being perfectly reasonable. He'd started it. Matt stated the facts to get them out of his system. It's up to her to think it over, or toss it away. She'd notice anyway; she's not stupid.

'It's a bad habit, I know.' That's it, try to make light of the situation. Leaning against the loose poles that hold up the swings, watching as the toes of her shoes scratch back and forth.

'Does it hurt?'

Staring. They're both just staring at each other. Maybe they both know that it was a stupid question, or maybe they're both thinking that it means more than they think it means. Maybe, *maybe*. His jacket sticks to the swing poles as his shoulder rises in a shrug, 'Sometimes.'

Taking up the swing next to her, neither of them really going anywhere. At least she's still here. There's nothing to make her stay. Round and round, Matt's feet push on the ground, careful that his hands don't get caught in the twisted chains. 'Depends. I have to be careful, y'know? Don't want it to hurt too bad.'

If she's saying anything he can't hear it, spinning round on the swing, feeling almost nauseous with the food he didn't have today. The chains pull and clank with the movement and weight before he judders to a stop. Pushing back the right sleeve of his coat, Matt's right arm is revealed. Looking at it beneath the orange lamplight it's almost completely normally. She'd have to look hard to really see the difference, but Matt pulls himself towards her swing anyway, jutting out the limb for her inspection.

'Right here.' His finger automatically points towards the puckered skin, watching her looking for something, but she doesn't know what it is.

'Skin graft.' Watching, waiting for some kind of signal of disgust. You'd expect a girl to look all sympathetic about it, but in experience they just looked creeped out. Maybe his story would be better if it involved a stabbing, or a shark, a rogue bullet or something. 'Had a bit of an accident involving a razor.' And that's why he rarely uses them anymore.

'Oh.'

He wants more than an 'oh', but she's twisting his arm, trying to catch a better light to examine the lines and scabs, 'Looks sore.'

'I can't even really feel it.' It was just an extra bit of skin, a part of a calf that no one saw anyway. He wasn't the type to feel the need to sunbathe in shorts.

She's still holding his arm, almost entranced by the thing. Just staring at it like she's expecting to find something there. There's no clue here, no arrows pointing to why. Eventually she lets go, carefully, like she's frightened she might drop it. He's not going to break, not that easily.

'I'm sorry.'

Matt laughs, comfortable, taking his withered arm back and hiding it again inside its sleeve.

'No worries. It wasn't your fault.'

That wasn't what she meant, but they both know that, sharing a silence that says "I know what you mean". Sarah's digging her hands into her pockets, producing a phone and pressing a button to light up the screen. 'What time is it?'

'Just about two.' She turns slightly, a hand covering her mouth to stifle a yawn. Too polite to say she doesn't want to be there.

'It's getting late. I'll walk you home?' He asks it like a question, too unsure to make it a statement. But she's already standing, waiting for him by the park gate. 'You know, you didn't have to come tonight.'

Sarah swings the gate open before inspecting her hands for flakes of blue paint. 'Look, like I said, I was happy to come out here. It was nice spending time with you.' Said like the most natural thing in the world. Sure, girls 'liked spending time with him', but that was usually said between sheets, or in other less fortunate places. Maybe, just maybe, she'd like to spend some time with him again, in that nice way. 'I mean, we'll meet up again soon, right?'

TEN

Sarah

Staring at my inbox, and the huge variation of notes never fails to fascinate me. Make a spreadsheet of the flowers wanted with the name of the person next to it. Done. Print it off, and take another look at the messages to go with the bouquets.

Sorry about that.
Jim.

Whatever he was sorry about, I'm really hoping it wasn't homewrecking. Maybe he's being funny, or maybe he's just insincere. What did he do? Run away with the office secretary. Dear wife, sorry about that. Sorry for turning your life into such a sad cliché.

Dear Angela,
I love you more than life itself. You mean the world to me.
Please will you marry me?
Yours forever,
Tom.

Wow. So Tom proposes with flowers. What did he choose? Oooh, the lovely winter special. Well, they always say to say it with flowers, and actually Laura's done a really good job with that one. Still, it would be nice if he could be a little more original. He means well though, and I'm sure Angela will appreciate it.

Dear Michelle,
Whoo hoo! You did it! We are so proud of you, our clever daughter.
Lots of love,
Mum and Dad.

That's sweet. Winter graduation is my guess. Or maybe she got a new job. So well done Michelle, you probably deserve it. At least your parents sound nice.

'Sarah, dear!' Laura's choked with a cold, and she has been for days. Her throat sounds like it's full of grit. 'Put the kettle on, dear!'

I call through, 'Okay!' but my voice is lost beneath the hissing of boiling water, already pre-emptive to Laura's morning routine of a hot drink. I always imagined Laura to be the type of person who has one of those Best Mum or My Wife mugs, the kind of thing men think is a 'nice' present from a card shop. Instead, she has a Charles

Rennie MacIntosh tea cup with that famous rose pattern on. It suits her. If someone were to send Laura some flowers, I wonder what the card would say. Does anyone actually send her flowers? No bouquets for the florist. But I bet her home is full of them, flowers dripping from the windowsills.

'Tea or coffee, or Lemsip?'

Laura's laughter is audible as she coughs between each breath, 'Just a camomile for me just now, please.'

It's like being in our own cosy little flower world, working here. I can see the downpour outside, and I can hear it rattle on the windows. But everything in here is bright and...flowery. It's not like a supermarket, or any other kind of shop. People don't come here because it's an everyday necessity, and people don't come here just because they feel like a browse. We get brides-to-be, new grandparents, anxious husbands and funeral directors. Everyone that comes through Laura's doors brings with them an agenda.

She's talking in hushed tones to a man with broad shoulders. He's considerably taller than both of us and the hair on his head is vanishing white. My smile is sympathetic as I set Laura's cup on the coaster by the till. We're trained in knowing what the customer is here for, and I'm pretty sure I'm right in assuming that the man is either recently widowed or knows someone who has died. Laura told me that it's awkward and unfair to ask what the occasion is. Better still, it's just good customer service. She prides herself on knowing what her customers want, and even learned to fine tune her gaydar so that she could recognise homosexuals and understand what flowers she should recommend for Valentine's Day.

Promptly I set to my calligraphy, but it doesn't take long. Time for my own cup of tea and figuring out her accounts. I feel like I'm reading someone's private bank statements, taking notes on what money's coming in and going out. Just Laura and me in the whole place, and out of that money come my wages and hers. She's not exactly rolling in it, but she makes a decent amount of profit. It's not bad work, and it keeps her comfortable; for 'nice things' as she says. Summers are weddings and winters are funerals and Christmas.

Joanna,
Lord bless you and keep you,
The Lord make His face to shine upon you,
And be gracious unto you.
The Lord lift up His countenance upon you,
And give you peace.
Numbers 6:24
Irma.

I like the flowers sent with religious verses; Christian sayings, and lines from the Qur'an, Jewish blessings for Jewish holidays. After this message is another.

Hi Mum and Dad!
Happy Hanukkah!
Be home soon to celebrate!
John.

Flicking through the calendar on my desk, I'm informed that Hanukkah starts in a few days. So good of their son to be punctual. Which means Naomi will probably be heading home soon for the holidays. Shit.

Without Naomi the flat is creepily empty. Moan as I might about having her around, it's weird when she goes. Just me in the morning, just me in the evening. Just me. Least I can get the bath whenever I want. I'll run up electricity bill keeping the TV on just for some background noise, the sound of someone else with me. Things are restless with all that city noise and students toing and froing from halls.

Laura appears by my desk and though she owns the place, she's twisting her hands like she's just intruded on my privacy. She has every right to be here. Smiles and soft voices comfort her. 'Hi', is as much as I say, though really 'What's wrong?' would be far more appropriate.

'Listen, why don't we close up early today, hmm? And let's just take tomorrow off.' It's only two in the afternoon, and wild eyes flash over the cards drying on the desk. She picks up the message from Irma, careful not to smudge the ink. Dry, cracked lips move soundlessly as her eyes travel over the words and a slow smile twitches over her face. 'Just get your stuff together and I'll lock up.'

Can't help but just stare while I shut down the computer, taking my eyes off her only to fish out my bag from beneath the table. Surface, and she's still standing, only this time her hands are pressed hard to her mouth and the veins of her hands stand out blue.

'Laura, are you okay? I mean, I can stay and lock up if you like.'

But I doubt she even hears me, her mind only processing her own thoughts. Her lips tremble, flicking from a smile to an open gape and the words that follow are heavy, like it hurts her to speak, 'That man was my brother. Father's passed away.'

Someone had died. Ready to leave, standing to give her a hug. She flinches, her protruding spine shaking, like every vertebrae is trying to go somewhere.

'I'll see you soon, then, hmm?' It's a cue for me to leave, so I leave her with a smile. Though I'm not sure what good that will do. Taking the prettiest bouquet I can find, I put £20 through the till and leave the white and purple flowers with a note. I'm not sure what I can say, so I scribble down a few words with a Biro.

Numbers 6:24.
Sarah x

Flowers for the florist.

ELEVEN

Matt

To say that Thursdays are quiet is an understatement. A big student night, so the usual customers hit the clubs and ignore the pubs. At the bar, Matt busies himself with cleaning and shining glasses. Hardly silver service, but they look better on the shelf when they're actually clean. The couple sitting in the window don't seem to object to the tracks he's playing on the jukebox. Songs click from one to the other, and as the next starts up there's a smile of recognition from both girls and they burst into laughter at the unspoken recollection of something fun.

The heavy doors swing open, bringing with them cold winter air and a figure wrapped up in a parka. Matt groans, shuffling to lean on the bar, already mixing up a Sailor Jerry's with Coke. 'What are you doing here?'

'Oh, just charming. Charming. No "nice to see you, Johnny." I've missed you too, mate.' Furry hood is pushed down to reveal Johnny's huge set of teeth.

'What kind of time is this?' Oh God. 9:15. Possible Sarah/Johnny clashing. Of all the days he could have showed up...

'Well, what? You're always telling me to come by the bar, and I come by and you don't even want me here.' Feigned pain and anguish crosses Johnny's face as he removes his glasses, wiping the steam with his sleeve. 'Anyway, Matty boy, how goes it?'

'It goes.' Matt places the drink in front of him, opening up his palm expectantly.

'Eh? You're expecting me to pay for shit now? C'mon, this is supposed to be my cheap night out.' All the same, the five pound note makes its way to Matt while Johnny slips onto a stool. 'So, I've got a job interview tomorrow, can you believe it?'

'Getting all respectable now, are we Johnny? Where for?'

'Greggs. How immense is that? I bet I'll get free yum yums and everything. Imagine, all the sausage and bean pasties you could eat.'

'You won't have your job long if you're eating all the stock. Besides, you'll get fat.'

Johnny looks down at his stomach, patting at it protectively, a small crease of worry on his forehead, 'Fuck, never thought about that. Ah well, I'll just take up smoking.' He grins with a straw between his teeth, like he's discovered the cure for obesity.

'Healthy, Johnny. Healthy.'

'So, you still with that girl from the party?'

Sarah... Matt's eyes flick to the clock above his head, the minute hand creeping steadily closer to the 6. Arms folded tightly about his chest, his back straightens, focusing on the beer tabs rather than looking at his friend, 'Her name's Sarah.'

'Holy hell!' Johnny leans so far back on his stool that he nearly falls off the thing, correcting himself in time to prevent his drink from spilling, 'This one has a name? Whoa, little Matty's getting serious.'

'Actually, she's coming here tonight. 'Bout five minutes.'

'Shit. Coming to see you at work too? Matt, you're whipped.' Johnny settles his feet on the spoke at the bottom of stool, ready for a good story. 'So, what's she like?'

Matt shakes his head, one hand clutching at the tufts of hair at the nape of his neck, 'We're not sleeping together, if that's what you mean.'

'Aww Matt,' Johnny wets his lips with his tongue before moving them into a pout. 'Is that really all I think about?' The moment their eyes meet the boys fall into laughter, both at themselves, and at each other. Knowing each other like they do, there's no need for second guessing. The doors are opening, another gust of air blowing through the warmth of the bar. But it's just a couple of guys, eyeing the place over like they've never been, registering the sofas and the wallpaper on their way to the bar.

'Eh, couplae pints ae...' He's eyeing the row of beer taps, 'Aye, couplae pints ae Stella.'

Johnny sips at his drink, smirking behind his straw while Matt pulls the pints. He sneaks a glance at the clock behind his head, so used now to serving his customers with minimum concentration. 'There you are.'

The guy reaches into his pockets, sifting through coppers to find some useful coins and passes them over to Matt. 'Cheers.'

'Oooh, quarter to ten. Doesn't look like your lady's gonna show tonight.' So, it isn't the most reassuring statement in the world, but at least there is some heartfelt warmth somewhere behind his words.

Still, it doesn't wash with Matt, and he's pulling his phone from his pocket, double checking the time. 21.44. More or less quarter to ten. But why wouldn't she come?

While the lesbian couple leave, one girl holds the door open for the next windswept stranger. Matt's practically beaming, his face visibly brightened, while throwing Johnny a triumphant I-told-you-so smile. Johnny meets it with an impressed nod, pretending to be any patron and poking at the melting ice in his glass with his straw.

'Hey, sorry I'm late. It's been a...interesting day.' Sarah's flustered, fumbling with her coat buttons, resting her umbrella beneath a stool and reaching into her little handbag all at once.

'That's okay, that's okay.' He's just glad that she's here, but all the same his ears are hot with the anticipation of the impending introduction. 'Uh, so, this is my friend Johnny. Y'know, the one I was looking for at the party.'

Pleased to be part of the conversation, Johnny slides his glass across the bar, 'Nice to finally meet you, Sarah -'

Matt knows by the tone of his friend's voice and the fiendish smile on his face that he has much more to say, but it's safer to cut him short before anything dangerous happens, 'What can I get you to drink?'

'Uhm...' She shifts in her stool, getting comfy on her jacket as it dangles beneath her, 'Just a bottle of -'

'Peroni.' Johnny says it just as the word comes from Sarah's own mouth. He raises a hand, waving away the embarrassed confusion flushing on her cheeks, 'Don't worry. I'm not reading your mind.'

Matt's inward groan becomes an outward sigh as he places the cold bottle in front of her, 'Tell me about your day.' Eyes bright, oblivious to the fact that the jukebox is silent now, waiting for a story.

'Well, you know that I work in the florist's, right? Well, Laura, my manager, her dad died today.' The bottle scrapes against the bar, and Sarah takes a slow sip, the guys averting their eyes while they wait for her to continue, 'Her brother came in to tell her. And she just closed the shop. So, I've got the day off tomorrow.'

Johnny leans to nudge at her arm, missing and elbowing her in the ribs, 'Ah well, least you get the day off. Long weekend - least that's something.'

Matt scowls with a hand gripped firmly on the bar edge. Just a flash of his eyes and Johnny knows his joke was misplaced, encouraging his friend to give an apologetic wave of his hand. 'I'm sorry to hear that.'

Rubbing tentatively at her ribs, Sarah just nods her head, shoulders lifting in a sigh, 'It's just weird. So unlike her to be that way. Poor Laura, she must be in so much shock. Least she has her brother. I thought she was totally alone.'

The man from before returns to the bar, digging a pile of money from his pocket and peeling away a blue five pound note, 'Same again, pal?'

'Yeah, sure.' Matt's hardly aware of what he's doing, trying to catch Sarah's eye and silently let her know that he's there, trying to throw a subtle smile towards Johnny, just to say he's pleased that he hasn't ruined anything. Yet.

The first pint he pulls is mostly froth, and it takes another slow attempt to get it right. 'There you are.' Busying about with the money and the till, he does his best to conceal his excitement in noticing that Johnny's pulling on his jacket.

'Right, think it's bedtime for this cowboy.' He casts a weary glance to windows by the door, trying to assess the rain situation through the darkness. 'Back in a bit.'

Both Matt and Sarah watch him swagger to the toilet before exchanging nervous smiles. Matt has to look professional. At least, as professional as the job of bartender requires. Still at work, still with customers to serve and floors to clean. Tonight, Sarah is just a customer. Just a customer he wants to pull round the bar and squeeze and tell that everything's going to be okay, that she can talk to him and that he's here for her. But instead he just keeps smiling.

'Right kids, I'm out of here!' Johnny's at the other end of the room, waving, a gig flyer in his hand. 'Sarah, make sure my boy stays out of trouble, okay?'

Matt gets in before Sarah has to trouble with a response, 'Aye, aye, okay. Just go to bed, Johnny.'

She's sipping on her bottle, and Matt's wondering what to say. Maybe if there was just the two of them, both drinking, anywhere else, it might be a different scenario. 'So, you have tomorrow off?'

'Yeah.'

'Well...want to do something through the day? Before I start my shift here?'

He's impressed at how much he manages to brighten up her face, making her lips curl into a relieved smile and her eyes soften. No way he's making this stuff up. Is the prospect of spending time with him really that exciting to her? God, he hopes so.

'Okay. What do you want to do?'

'Lunch. Let's have lunch. We'll have a picnic, go to the park. Take a blanket and everything.' A little carried away with his idea, because he knows that in his head it sounds like a winner.

But his suggestion is met with laughter, not awe and excitement. He's pretty sure she's not actually laughing at him. Maybe.

She mops a drop of beer from her lips with a finger, 'Have you seen the weather out there?'

In all honesty it had occurred to him, though not in a practical sense. He envisages hot chocolate on the swings, kisses in the rain on the roundabout. Way too much of a hopeless romantic. 'So? It'll be nice. A winter stroll.' He savours the last three words, presenting them with flourish like bait.

Sarah licks the remainder of her drink from her lips, raising a brow at Matt's wide eyes and boyish determination, 'Alright. Sounds good.'

Whether she is imagining the same scenario that he was is irrelevant now. Time to worry about where to buy food, what to buy, if he could really use that blanket in the cupboard or if it still stinks of stale whisky. 'Great! So, how bout I meet you here tomorrow say...twelve? Then we can go to Tesco or whatever and see what we can get? Pork pies are a must, by the way.'

'Definitely. And Scotch eggs.'

Matt pulls at face at her suggestion, but noting the arch in her eyebrows he tugs a hand through his hair. 'Sure thing, Scotch eggs and all.' He watches as she gathers up her little bag, digging through for her purse. The one she had last time, and he smiles at the little recognition, beginning to remember details about her that maybe no one ever noticed. Her hand is held open in front of him, a collection of one and two pound coins. It's only after too many moments that he clicks that she's trying to pay for the drink. Boldness takes over, and his hand meets hers, gently curling her fingers back over her money, careful not to break them.

'It's on the house.' With just a soft smile and the slightest of bows, because it's best not to upset the other customers; staunch neds with bad haircuts can't expect the same treatment.

TWELVE

Sarah

The point of winter accessories is to look cute and feel cosy at the same time. Choosing the right scarf and deciding between mittens or fingerless gloves is crucial. If I chose the mittens this morning, there would definitely be no chance for holding hands, and I'd fumble over the picnic food. If I chose fingerless my fingers would be too icy to touch. So it's just plain old gloves, boring red hands and red fingers. They match my red duffel coat, which matches my brown ankle boots, which match the black knee high socks, which look really cute with my winter dress. Not that anyone can see it, but I know that I'm wearing it and I know that it looks great. As great as it's going to.

But did I choose the right colour of eyeshadow? Should I have gone for a cream that won't melt? If it rains will my waterproof mascara run? Maybe if my face starts to melt it'll look sweet, like I'm washing away in the rain. Or maybe I'll look like Grizabella's ugly understudy.

If this was our first time meeting, there's no way I'd agree to this. In the shop window is a girl that could be cuddly all wrapped up, but she's probably just really frumpy and hiding her fat thighs. Taking advantage of the weather to conceal stomach fat and boobs that could probably do with being bigger, or rounder. Or smaller, like a model's; those girls can wear anything.

He's gone for cosy and cute too, chatting to someone on his phone outside his pub. He's noticed me, smiling for all the world, and I'm checking myself over to make sure nothing's out of place. If it is, he doesn't seem to have noticed, as he mouths 'I've got to go. Chat soon.'

'Hey Sarah, how are ya?' Finding it difficult to see past his smile, but he's taking hold of my gloved hand. He opted for fingerless, and I wish I had too. His free hand pats at the leather satchel hanging by his hip, 'Got a blanket, a full flask, and some whisky too. Just in case.'

Urgh, whisky. I don't even know if I don't like it, it's just one of those things that probably wouldn't agree with me. The smell definitely doesn't.

'Sounds...cosy.'

But I'm trying to be positive all the same. I'm really going to be. *Have* to be. No one wants to hang around with a wet drip. Right now I'm just so glad it isn't raining. There are big black clouds lumping over the rooftops, so it's going to happen soon. Looking for a silver lining; it's got to be somewhere.

Picking up a basket at Tesco, looking at the printed receipt left in it: milk, three crates of Strongbow, Rice

Krispies, Value chocolate. Who would guess we're bang in the middle of a student city?

'Okay, so what do we need?'

He's saying something, hand tugging as I'm guided round the place. Don't know how many times I've shopped here but the aisles are always different, jumbled up and never in any kind of sensible order. Matt looks at me and smiles, so I return the gesture. Just making sure I'm still with him. I'm here, but desperate to perform some kind of disappearing act. Pretty, skinny girls all over the shop. Immaculate hair, skin, clothes. Laughing in groups, clutching baskets full of herbal teas and slimming cereal. Raindrops glistening in their hair and unadulterated happiness shining in their smiles. I bet they read *Elle* and take fashion tips from *Vogue*, they're well versed in poetry but everything they know about life they learned from Shakespeare. They have sensitive skin, but take regular trips to Verona. One girl is looking at me, a hummingbird pendant dangling in the front of her Merino cardigan. Baby pink. She's looking at the cheeses again, but she sized me up in a second: a dysfunctional girl from a dysfunctional family, a mediocre degree with a useless job to show for it. What am I doing with this boy? He could be doing so much better.

Matt

Staring at the cheese for what seems like forever, picking up a slab labelled Roquefort, poking at the green veins through plastic wrap. Why can't she just pick up some cheddar and have this over and done with? Supermarket shopping was a good idea at the time, because that's what couples do. He trusts her to make informed decisions about food, leaving their entire meal to her own devices. Matt takes the basket from her arm, like playing one of those metal buzzer games. She leans, scarf dangling over the mozzarella while she's umming and hmming between mild and mature.

'Let's just take both. They're on offer.' As much advice as he's ready and willing to give and fortunately it's greeted with an easy smile, basket weighing in his hand with two blocks of cheese.

There are people in Tesco. Groups of people, loud people, bodies and voices everywhere, and nowhere to turn. All baskets, and trolleys, ridiculously large handbags and children. Running children. Where are their parents? This one has wheels on her heels, shouting to her friend in the next aisle. She doesn't know where the sugar is. She can't find the sugar. Okay, her friend says, it's over here. Where? Over *here*. Next to the flour. The whole of the supermarket really doesn't need to know. Meanwhile, there's a couple buzzing around the cold meats, whispering threats and angry accusations. Too much drama, too much noise. Matt's basket bashes into the ribs of the surly man in question, his red face still bright from the annoyance brought on by his wife who is going to go and find the beetroot anyway. The man's mouth twists like he's sucking on lemons, a soft eff ready to turn into something harsher. But Matt hurries his 'Sorry,' navigating his way between the angry man and a woman with a buggy and screaming two year old. No, he can't have a magazine.

Panting by the fabric conditioner, a sour-sweet smell drifting from powder spilled and scattered at his feet. Sarah's flushed, dropping chicken and tuna sandwich fillers into the basket.

'Sorry, I couldn't find you.' Making the situation look like confusion, reaching for some Jammy Dodgers on the promotion aisle-end.

'Huh? I was right beside you.' Sarah's confusion more genuine, failing to understand how he'd lost her when she was holding onto his hand.

'Oh, yeah. Let's get some bread.' He squeezes her hand determined that she shouldn't lose him again. Two French bread batons, flung into the basket to complete the picnic, with some double chocolate muffins just for good measure. 'These are really good,' he promises.

Queuing is half the battle, just shuffling and kicking the basket along; standing helpless amidst the chaos of people.

Self-service is safer. Just beep the stuff through and put it in a bag. Go home without having to communicate with anyone. No awkward questions about packing bags and Clubcards. Sarah puts the items through the scanner, and Matt packs them into flimsy carrier bags, strategically distributing weight. There's nothing worse than bursting a bag and having the contents smashed all over the pavement. People stare, smile sadly, and there's always the inevitable, 'Wahey' that comes from somewhere in a flat window overhead. Please take your items, the machine lady says, and Matt grabs at the bags, almost missing a handle and causing the worst. Through the automatic door and he breathes in the cigarette clouds of workers on a smoke break. Something fluffy brushes his hand, the touch reminding him that he'd left Sarah behind.

The streets are quiet, shoppers and students turned off the street with the prospect of rain. It's a good excuse to save some money, and a good excuse to not attend a lecture. No one seems to be going anywhere, footsteps only rushing to escape a down pour.

'I can't believe I forgot my umbrella.'

Matt pauses, eyes scanning over Sarah's face; words bitter from a little mouth. His fingers clutch tighter at her woollen knuckles and he makes a brave step towards the traffic lights, pressing the wet button and waiting for green. They're making their way along the streets, moving quickly before the bags break, small tears already showing in the plastic.

'Don't worry, we'll find cover.'

The park is empty, not even suitable for an alcoholic's needs in this weather. Rain drops heavy and fat from dark clouds, spreading and consuming any spare space of grey. Blue to grey, grey to black. With the climbing frame as den, Matt claims his space with a tartan rug, pressing down on rough bark chips and smoothing out the lumps.

'There.' Triumphant, a king in his newly conquered castle. With his queen. She's crouching in the entrance, watching him prepare for the picnic, all house-proud and pleased. 'Come on in.' He's already pulling things out of bags, setting lunch out between them as he tucks his legs beneath him.

Carefully he breaks off some baguette, silently noting the distinct lack of cutlery, and using a piece of crust to spread coronation chicken. Matt takes a bite, painfully aware of the way that he chews, eyes watching for food falling on his chest.

'Could you please pass me the tuna?'

He swallows, wiping away crumbs that stick to his gloves, before picking up the small tub and handing it across the blanket as she crawls in and settles down.

Sarah

There's no way I can open the cheese, not with these gloves on, and not while I'm shaking so hard. It's freezing, seriously cold. Though it seemed like a good idea at the time. Can whisky really taste all that bad? Really struggling to make any kind of decent sandwich here. Maybe I can get away with just scooping the stuff out of the tub. It works. Taking tiny bites, chewing slowly. I have no idea what I look like when I eat; one of the few things that I haven't tried in the mirror.

'Want some tea?'

So glad he asked that, but my mouth is full so I nod like an idiot in response. The water's still hot and I can feel the warmth through the plastic cup. Almost burning my throat, I drink it quickly to savour the heat in my stomach, willing it to spread to my lungs and my feet.

'You know, when I younger I used to think that tuna was made out of dolphins. Figured that's why the tins all said "Dolphin Friendly" on them.'

I think about this, pausing to look at the tuna on my bread, but my laughter comes out in a burst. Lucky that my mouth was empty because otherwise the scenario would have been worse than it is.

'Really?' Not sure if this is a genuine anecdote from his youth, or just some kind of humorous story he's picked up along the way.

He studies the Jammy Dodger in his hand, breaking it in half and watching the jam stretch,

'Yup, really. My friend came back from Florida with pictures of Sea World. I was pretty confused, so I asked the teacher what parts they used and how come they got it so small in the tins.'

Shuffling, I rescue my legs from cramp, stretching them across the width of the climbing frame to touch the other side.

Donna n Daz 4 Eva. I.D.S.T.

'Aww bless. So what did your teacher say?'

'She very politely showed me an encyclopedia we had in the class and found the page with tuna fish. I was still pretty confused, y'know, cause tuna are pretty big.'

'Okay, and when was this? Higher geography?'

The way he lowers his head in mock shame is just too amusing to watch, complete with hiding behind his hands, eyes peeking out between fingers. 'Yeah.' Matt reveals his face to the darkness of our den, grin stretching from one ear to the other, 'Nah, really, was primary seven.'

Laughing again, kicking my feet to keep the warmth going. Curiosity and nosiness allowing me to watch as he removes the whisky from his bag and starts to pour a small amount into a cup. My staring hasn't gone unnoticed, and he's lifting the bottle, shaking it like he's enticing a dog to a treat, 'Want some?'

'Suppose it wouldn't hurt to try.'

'You don't like it?' Passing me the cup he's just poured, getting another from his bag to measure more for himself.

'Never really tried it. Kind of thing that gets my mum and my uncle really drunk at parties. And their breath *stinks*, so I try to avoid it.'

'They brother and sister?'

The way my head's shaking, it's in dismay rather than in answer, 'Nope. Mum, and Dad's brother.'

'Oh...'

It's a touchy subject with Dad, but Matt's giving a smile like he knows what it's like. But I wonder if his family is remotely as crazy as mine. I hope to God not. 'Yeah, makes Christmas really...special.'

'I bet.' He sips at his drink and just smiles, nodding to encourage me to do the same.

What the hell is this stuff? It catches the back of my throat, and my tongue feels like it's on fire. A really sour, bitter, yucky fire. Appalled, my tongue's hanging out my mouth now, like the cold weather will make it better.

Matt's laughing at me, but maybe with me too, raising his brows over the rim of his cup, a scoff echoing inside the plastic.

It's all I can do but reach for a Jammy Dodger in the hope that it'll help revive my taste buds. 'Mum's coming to stay soon. She wants me to go home for Christmas but...

it's gonna be so weird and pretty shit without Dad there.' I don't know what made me say it, but I shove the biscuit in my mouth and bite hard to stop me saying anything more.

'How are they?'

It's been a while since I've mentioned anything to do with the divorce. Talking about things always makes things seem more real, like if you keep them bottled up inside then no one ever needs to know about it. 'Well, Dad seems to be AWOL. I can't get him on his phone, and he hasn't emailed me. I mean, I haven't emailed him either but he said that he would be in touch. Mum reckons he's got a toy boy in Hawaii but -'

'Oh, it's like that is it?'

'I don't even know.' And I don't. It's as likely true as it's likely false. The taste of this whisky is preferable to having to think about the impending visit from Mum. I try it again with just the tip of my tongue, but it's the smell that hits me first. Maybe if I hold my nose.

'Hey, it's okay. If you don't like it you don't have to drink it.'

'No, no. It's...okay.' My smile is weak. I can feel the corners of my lips drooping, like one of those theatre masks. My eyes feel like they're melting too, rain drops soaking into my eyelashes and settling heavily round the edges of eyeliner. There's nothing surrounding us that I can check my face with, and it would just look weird or conceited or both to start digging around for my mirror. 'So, what are *your* plans for Christmas?' Get the onus away from me.

'Just staying here.' He's reaching for the bread, tearing at the crust without remorse. 'Working.' Shrugging, like it's no biggie, but his shoulders sag with an invisible weight.

'What about Christmas dinner and stuff? Seeing your family?' Really, I have no idea where his family live or what they do. Posing questions that might give me the answers, without appearing too nosey.

'Nah. Things are...weird at home.' The piece of bread he's holding is broken in half again, and he brushes the crumbs off his jeans with the back of his hand.

'Oh.'

'Yeah. I mean, basically, I'm not the most welcome guest at home. Mum's ill, Dad's...well, he's Dad. And my sister pretty much doesn't ever want to talk to me.' Stuffing his face with cold meats, and I can't help but watch the rigidity of his jawline while I wait for more. But it's not offered. Don't think it will be.

'Oh. Not so good, then?' That's it Sarah, just try and make light of a situation that is quite clearly horrible. Brush over it like you never asked. How tactful.

'Not really.' Voice distant, eyes blurred. I've opened the key to something he's been hiding, but before I can continue to make stupid comments, he's leaning back against the wall of the frame, turning his head toward me. 'But no worries. I'm gonna win the lottery next weekend. Twice. National and Euromillions. Then I'll buy me a huge villa in California. Beach parties every day, and all the best people in the world will be there.'

'Really? Who will you invite?'

Matt's thought about this too much, no way is his answer prepared on the spot, 'The usual. Bono, Stephen Fry, Christian Bale, Lord Sugar.'

'Christian Bale?'

'Don't judge. Ever seen *American Psycho*?'

I shake my head. One of those films and books that's referenced everywhere that I know nothing about. I feel shamefully down on my pop culture.

'Yeah, well.' Matt grins, continuing his list like it was never interrupted, 'Christina Ricci, Katy Perry, The Queen.'

'The "best people in the world"?' Best people in the world, and the kind that I could never contend with. Twisting at the ends of my hair, wishing that I was -

'Who would you invite?'

'Hmm? Oh. Uhm... Do they have to be living?'

'Yup. The dead party is a different question.'

'Oh, okay. I'd invite...Audrey Tautou, Johnny Depp and... Derren Brown.'

Matt laughs, but it's appreciative, I think. 'That would be some party.' He shakes his head, 'Aw man, the conversations going on at that party... Pretty weird.'

'Well...I suppose.' Maybe I've done something wrong. Maybe in choosing these people I've unwittingly exposed or revealed something about my personality, about my head. Maybe now I'm just 'weird'.

'Still, not any weirder than mine, I guess.' His smile gleams as he licks his teeth with his tongue, cleaning them of whisky drops. 'But it's good to think about these things. You never know when you're going to make it big, right?'

'What are you going to make it big with?'

'After I've won the lottery, everyone's gonna want to know me. Everyone's gonna want to be my friend. They'll say, "Hey, Matt, what do you do in your 'spare time'?" And I'll say, "Well, why don't you take a look at my photography exhibition?" And they'll love it, everyone telling me that I'm a genius and why didn't people know this before.'

Matt bubbles with enthusiasm, like a boiling pot of potentiality. So much going on beneath the surface that he wants to get out. And here, beneath the climbing frame and the rain, I catch a glimpse of it. 'Okay, and I can write really wanky reviews about your photographs and talk about light and metaphors and...*art*.'

'Absolutely.' He raises a hand and I lift mine, meeting his quickly to smack with a high five, but quicker than that his fingers catch mine, curling my hand into his.

***

'Aww, cute, I have a son now.' I pick up a blue peg and press it gently into the little plastic car. My family is arranged so that my eldest, a daughter, sits behind the father, and the new born son sits behind the mother, me.

'Congratulations! Now you're a national average.' Matt grins as he reaches over to spin for his turn. In his car are two pink pegs, choosing a lesbian lifestyle.

'And you're probably some kind of statistic too, so good for you.'

He shrugs and moves his car forward, 'I probably go to more parties than you, though.'

'So? I have love and fulfilment. And a career as an artist. I feel blessed to have little Lisa and Johnny in my life.'

Matt scratches an eye as he looks down at the board, 'You can't call our kids after our friends.'

'Oh...so their our kids now, are they?' I'm teasing, but I can feel my cheeks flush, and not at the expense of my glass of wine. The concept of children has never included an 'our' before.

He shakes his head and takes a sip from his beer,

rubbing his lips together, 'I guess. Unless you want to be off having them with someone else.'

'Well, I'm not having any today. Or tomorrow.'

Matt holds my gaze for long enough that it's almost uncomfortable, and I hope he'll be the first to look away. He does, and points to the spinner, 'Your turn.'

The conversation has passed, he seems intent on just getting on with the game. But he's there in front of me, Matt, a possible future. 'D'you think you want kids? I mean, not necessarily with me, but I mean, one day?'

'I don't know. It's a nice idea, but I don't think I'm cut out for it.'

'Why not?'

He fingers through his paper money, 'I dunno. I think I'd leave them in the car with the windows up or something.'

It's so cute, the way he says it, like maybe he's really concerned about this, and I can't help but laugh, 'I was asking about children, not dogs.'

Matt pulls a face before finishing his beer. He places the empty bottle beside another on my bedroom floor. 'One day, I'm sure it'll be all I want. An actual family. But not for...at least ten years. I'll be mid-thirties by then, so my life will be pretty much over anyway.'

'Hmm...' The idea of being in my thirties seems odd as it is; I'm not sure what I'm supposed to achieve between now and then. 'Well, all I know is that I'd rather not be a granny before I get pregnant.'

'A granny first? Yeah, that's a bit backwards.'

My arm reaches out, not to hit him, just a playful touch to his arm, while I laugh, 'Yeah, okay.'

Matt looks at me steadily with a slow smile, 'It's still your turn.'

So I spin the dial, move some spaces, and land with, 'Ski accident. Pay $5000.' My money is depleting, but I grudgingly take the paper from my pile, 'Here you go, doctor.'

'Thanks, patient. Though you're lucky, affording to go skiing when you have two kids. Especially a newborn.'

'But when you're one part of a lesbian couple you can do what you want?'

He takes the money and bundles it together, not in any kind of organised way, 'Basically. Why play *Game of Life* when you could play *Jumanji*? No kids means no responsibilities. Your life is ruined now.'

This isn't supposed to be serious, but I'm frowning, and close to throwing my car across the board. Maybe every parent makes jokes about how much better their life was before them, how much freer they were, but for all Mum's lies and false compliments, sentences beginning with 'before you' or 'without you' seem too honest. 'Yeah, it is.'

'Hey, what's up?' Matt's leaning across the game, trying to find a place to rest his palm that won't disrupt the pieces.

'Nothing. It's just, thinking about stupid things Mum has said.' Looking down at the board, at the coloured roads leading round and round, past colleges and universities, leading to retirement.

'No offence, Sarah, but she doesn't sound like the sharpest tool in the box. I'm sure she doesn't really mean a lot of these things. Not in a nasty way.' His hand lifts from the board and rests on my thigh.

'Yeah. Probably.' But with Mum I always feel like the things she says mean more, because she hasn't tried to hide behind any cryptic words.

'Either way, I know I'm very happy that you exist.'

I lift my eyes to see Matt's face close to mine; eyes wide, blue, and eager, his lips finding mine. Something plastic snaps as we fall into one another. There's a hand on my back, and a hand on my thigh, and I'm holding his shoulders. Hot warmth and a thudding in my chest. Just a kiss but I can feel it tingle in my toes. Matt pulls gently away and brushes my fringe from my eyes. I feel like I should say something, something witty and cute, or else true and meaningful. Searching his face for clues of what happens next, his lips, his nose, his lips, his eyes.

I kiss him again, wanting and wanted.

THIRTEEN

Sarah

'Darling, darling,' words punctuated with kisses and heavy Gucci scents, 'the taxi driver took me everywhere, must have taken me for some kind of tourist.' Her voice gets higher, faster, and louder as she continues to gush about her journey; a warbling crescendo. I'm being pushed into the corridor, trying to make room for a mass of scarves and luggage. She's peeling off her coat, holding it out at arm's length so that I can have the pleasure of hanging it up somewhere for her. Flung in the ironing cupboard, it's now clothing the stepladders.

'Well, well? How have you been?' Wide brown eyes, depressingly similar to mine, wildly taking in the small space while she tries to remember the layout of the property that *she* bought, opening the toilet door before finding the living room. Plopping down on the sofa, she raises her head like an incensed peacock, 'Anyway, dear, the flight was terrible. Do you have some wine?'

Speaking to Mum is like listening to her stream of thoughts; never thinking before she says any of it. It just comes pouring out as soon as it comes into her preened little head. Speaking to Mum isn't speaking at all. There's nothing conversational about it, no dialogue. Two bottles, two glasses fetched from the kitchen and placed for her inspection on the coffee table. She's engulfed by pillows and unnecessary layers of clothing, but she steals herself from their suction to grab at a bottle. 'Oh *dear*, is this *really* what you drink?'

'Yes, Mum, it's *really* what I drink.' And there's absolutely nothing wrong with it. So it's a screw top cap, but why pay double for something that tastes just the same? Pouring white grenache into a glass (at least she got a reasonably clean one), sitting on the edge of the armchair. All of a sudden I can't relax in my own home, because it's *not* my own home, not when she's here.

What a joke: she's taking a sip, pencilled eyebrows arched like she's horrified at the taste. She always looks surprised with those brows but this is really taking the piss. But she's drinking it anyway. Half the glass at once. Dabbing at the corners of her greasy lips (a great plumper, she says, and really I should try some),

'Well, I was thirsty.' Always trying to justify herself. 'Honestly. Too terrible. You know that I booked with that Ryan Air or whatever they call themselves. Just couldn't think about being stranded somewhere awful with those British Airways strikes.'

'You flew here?' Where the hell was she?

'Well, of course.' And it occurs to her that I'm not always best informed of her whereabouts, 'London. I was in London, visiting friends.'

What friends? But I don't want to know, so I don't ask. I just sip slowly, making the wine last longer.
'Oh.'

'So, have you been busy, Sarah? You really ought to think about moving out of here. Get a real life.'

'And what exactly is a 'real' life? Drinking and shopping and divorce?' The words come out before I can stop them. She's making me nervous, and it's the first time I've seen her since she delivered the 'news'. I'm not team anyone any more.

'*Sarah*!' Mum's half way through her second glass already. 'No need for *bitter*ness. And it's perfectly healthy to *enjoy* life. I haven't enjoyed time with your father in years. Or -' All that's left of her wine are just drops on the side of the glass, sliding down to her fingers 'Or maybe ever.'

Who is this visit for? We'll celebrate for Christmas, she said, and have some girly time together. I think she had me confused with one of these 'friends' she seems to have acquired. Life is all one big episode of *Sex and the City* for Mum now. But I really, really don't need to know about the former part. Just Mum and the City. Safe.

'We can go to the Christmas market tomorrow. See the shows, get some mulled wine and stuff.'

'Do they still have a stall with those *delicious* crepes? We can get some and go laugh at the skaters before we go for a manicure. I need a manicure.' Twisting the metal cap on the next bottle, a Finest Chardonnay, she's inspecting her cuticles. 'Oh!' Eyes lighting up as she lifts her eyes to the room, 'Where are your decor*ations*, Sarah? We can get decorations, candles, and matching Christmas manicures. Green and red. Gold and red.'

'Green and red. With sparkles.' Shoulders shrugging back into the sofa, kicking off holey slippers. I always take great care of my nails, even if the red colour is chipped. But she has to be taking the piss. Is this what mothers and daughters do? Book candy cane manicures together?

Heavy heels clatter on laminate flooring, and I can't help but tilt my head to try to read the labels on the inside. Bare feet belonging to my mum, belonging to the shoes, return across the floor, flanked by fancy shopping bags of printed recycled paper and card stuffed with tissue paper. Distinctly not average high street; no twisted plastic handles in sight. 'Merry Christmas. Of course, you have to wait. Don't spoil the surprise. But you must, must, take a peek in here.' She pulls out a long thin box, lifting the top lid and smiling smugly. I'm supposed to be excited, so I lean forward slightly in my chair. But she snaps it shut, pressing her hand down hard for effect, 'Not until Christmas, Sarah. Not until *Christmas*.'

The not-to-be-opened-until-Christmas mantra doesn't fill me with the same excitement that it used to. Not Mum lying across the sofa in some flimsy silk present from Dad. Not Dad at the ready with a pack of batteries and a screwdriver, just in case. Not a champagne breakfast. Not Mum and Dad disappearing somewhere in the house while I'm busy with selection boxes and Barbie.

'And this is from your dad.' Voice flat, monotone and a small white envelope is held loosely between two fingers. She can't even look at it, tossing it over to land by my knee.

It is his handwriting, my name scribbled across the front with FAO sketched into the top left hand corner. A business transaction. My finger slips beneath the fold of the flap, but it's probably not a good idea. I don't know what's in here, and maybe I should find out later, though it's thin enough just be a cheque. 'Not until Christmas, I suppose', and making a point of putting the envelope on the edge of the sofa. Trying a smile, even though she's examining her iPhone now, acrylic nails tapping at the screen. 'Doesn't it scratch?'

Her lips purse and she makes a noise that I'm assuming means no, her head remaining still as she taps and taps and slides. 'Listen, dear,' the phone is placed gently on her knee, and she flicks away a stray thread, 'I'm meeting a friend for dinner this evening. An old school friend, you see, who I haven't seen in *such* a long time. You understand. But we can do cocktails later?'

Mum's voice inflects and her arched brow arches, but there's no question involved. She's got her plans, and those are what we stick to. 'Sure.'

'*Great.* Well, I'll just give you a text or a call when I'm done, and you can come meet me. Balmoral Hotel. I'll get you at the bar, yes?'

'Sounds great.' Sounds like Mum being drunk, me being tipsy. The wrong things said, the wrong things meant, me folding Mum into a taxi and bundling her into the flat, into bed. Morning and she'll take us for a fry up, like she's doing me a favour.

Already, she's slipping her feet back into those heels, grinning like an excited teenager when her phone vibrates, eagerly leering over the screen. Whoever, whatever. 'I'll see you soon then, yes? And if you're struggling for something to wear, just *treat* yourself to your Christmas presents early.'

FOURTEEN

Matt

Girls live here. It is quite obvious to Matt as soon as he walks over the threshold, just as striking as the first time he visited. Smells of vanilla candles, blinking fairy lights in doorframes, conversations from *Hollyoaks* drifting from a television. It's evident. Nice place though, in that pastel prairie kind of way.

'You remembered the buzzer number!' Sarah greets him with a pat on the arm, her other hand clutching a blanket round her shoulders.

'Yeah, I'm that good.' Fumbling with the buttons on his coat, Matt elbows around the small entrance, 'And I had it saved on my phone.'

Sarah stretches to open a small cupboard, shuffling in fluffy slippers; he's pretty sure there's supposed to be some kind of animal face on the toes but it's impossible to make out,
'I can put your jacket up in here, if you want.'

Matt smiles, ready to reply, when Sarah's flatmate creeps out of the kitchen. She looks busy, cheeks flushed and arms full of dry laundry, 'Oh, sorry. Excuse me.' Trying to get past with her arms wide, bed sheets and denim legs dangling.

'You must be Naomi.' Beaming, like a man who knows exactly how to present himself. 'I'm Matt. I'd shake your hand but I think it's lost in all that washing.'

The girl pauses, mouth parted and moving soundlessly until finally a whispered sentence rushes out, 'That's okay, just packing anyway, getting the train soon.'

Matt and Sarah exchange glances in the corridor, both matching, both different. Either way, mutually and silently agreeing to head into the living room. Matt flops down on Sarah's usual seat, so she opts for Naomi's sofa, picking up the remote to toss it on Matt's chest. 'We don't have to watch *Hollyoaks.*'

'No worries. It's...amusing. And there's always Jon Snow afterwards. I like his ties.'

'Wait til you see them on this TV; the colours are horrific.'

Naomi shuffles into the room, and Sarah has to scoot along the couch to give her space to sit. They're all silent, three sets of eyes staring at the screen but the likelihood is that no one's watching. Matt faces the television, kicking off his shoes to stretch his legs along pink and purple sequinned cushions, but his gaze moves to the DVD collection beneath the television. Black spines with gothic titles in white, red or green; a whole bunch of crazy Asian horror films. Next to some *House* boxsets and a cuddly toy cat. 'So, Naomi, what is it you do?'

'Psychology. Masters.'

'Really?' Matt twists round on his cushion, turning to give Naomi his attention. He gathers his legs, crossing them beneath him, 'Sounds interesting.'

Naomi responds to his beaming smile with a soft one of her own, nodding demurely like accepting a compliment. 'What about you?'

Sarah's eyes follow the ad on screen, but she drowns out the noise, pushing at the mute button on the remote.

'Freelance photographer. I work in a bar, but that's just to keep food on the table, ya know?' Matt leans, inspecting a hole on the toes of his socks, 'Uni wasn't really my thing.'

'So what brought you to Edinburgh?' A reasonable question from Naomi by all accounts. People were either born in Edinburgh or they moved for study or work.

'Just the right size for me, I guess. Didn't want to move back home so I came here.'

'Back home? From where?' Naomi watches Matt like watching the movements of a cat, grabbing a small purple bottle from the coffee table. Carefully, she unscrews the lid, only taking her eyes from him to make sure she didn't make a mess.

'Travelling.'

Hand flat against her thigh, Naomi flicks the brush along her nail, colouring her finger tips a pastel shade of lilac. 'Where did you go?'

'Round America. Went south for a bit too. Costa Rica, and that kinda thing.' Matt smiles across at Sarah, much amused at all the sudden curiosity: it's not everyday people care enough to ask about his adventures.

'Want some tea? Then you can tell us all about it.' Rousing out of her cosy position, Sarah pulls herself to standing.

'Water, please, is fine. Not a fan of tea.'

Sarah and Naomi's gasps come harmoniously and they exchange a look of shock regarding Matt's clearly ridiculous opinion.

The kettle clicks and hisses in the kitchen, tea cups rattling against their neighbours in the cupboard. Naomi glances at Matt over the top of her nails, inspecting what is far from a professional manicure. 'Some of my friends from school went there. Costa Rica.'

'Yeah? Nice place.'

'Mmhmm. They were doing conservation work. Housing turtles. Or helping them get to the sea. Or something.'

'I did some of that.' Matt sits up, carefully taking his glass from Sarah. She's juggling two cups of tea in the other hand, one of the cups tilting gradually closer to the floor. 'Careful.' But just as Matt utters his warning, a fat drop of tea falls on Sarah's foot, soaking into the eye of a slipper dog.

Her smile is accepting as she kneels to carefully place the cups on some coasters, mopping up any spillage with her finger. 'Don't worry. They're old anyway.'

'They really are. She's had them for so long there are holes in the bottom.' Naomi's voice is teasing though somewhat bashful as she dips her head, eyes travelling to seek out the damage on the slipper.

Sarah's already removing it from her foot, running her fingers through the matted hair of the ear, a thumb dabbing at the sinking tea stain. She turns it over in her hands, face falling to realise just how bad the hole was – material tearing away from material, ripping apart from the insole.

'Haha!' Matt's voice trumpets into the glass he's drinking from, 'You weren't kidding there, Naomi.' Satisfied, he leans back into the sofa, though not without offering a smile of condolence towards Sarah, 'Don't worry, I'm sure Santa can fix you up with some new ones.'

Sarah's eyes roll with impatience, and she sinks back into the sofa, cradling her mug between her hands, constantly shifting so her palms don't burn.

'"Santa" has already been, and I refuse to wear anything that "he" brought me.'

The comment meets Naomi's grimace, and Matt accepts it with a sorry smile; he still hasn't had the chance to catch up with Sarah on just how damaging "Santa's" visit was. So he draws a soft breath in through his teeth, nearly producing a whistling effect, and presses on with the small talk of conversation.

'You heading home for Christmas, then, Naomi?'

Examining some split ends, she's caught out by his address to her, sure she's playing the third wheel, the odd one out in their conversation.

'Hanukkah.' Naomi corrects him gently, her face twisting into an expression that resembles something like a smile.

'Yeah, of course.' And he's sorry because he's sure that somewhere along the line Sarah has mentioned this. Hence the conversation they'd had about Sarah celebrating Passover with Naomi's family earlier in the year, but secretly sharing Easter eggs anyway. 'So I'm guessing you're loads closer to your family than me or Sarah?'

'You could say that.' Naomi glances at her wristwatch, a kid's watch with a purple flower design. 'Anyway, I need to go grab my stuff and head for the train.' Having announced her departure, she stands and shifts through the space between the sofas.

Matt murmurs an 'alright', blue eyes finding Sarah's across the room. He holds her gaze, smiles softly, and can't help but be bewildered by her collapse into giggles. 'What's so funny?' Keeping his voice down, though Naomi probably can't hear between the wall, above the sounds of heavy suitcases.

Sarah just shakes her head, unable to pick up her mug for fear of spillage amidst the laughter, 'Nothing. Nothing.' But her throat is cleared as Naomi appears in the doorway, coated and hatted and gloved, trailing a case in each hand.

'Want a hand with that?' Matt shuffles to the end of the sofa, turning to assess the situation with a hint of genuine concern in his voice.

'No, it's okay. They're not that heavy. But thanks.'

'I'll get the door for you.' Sarah passes Matt, pointedly not looking at him and stifling a laugh. Two girly voices drift from the hallway, Sarah wishing Naomi a happy Hanukkah as she plays with the keys in the lock. Naomi says that she hopes she has a nice Christmas, trailing off like she's sure it's not going to be so straightforward. Muffled exchanges are made and faces buried in each other's shoulders in a hug.

'Bye Matt. Nice meeting you. Have a nice Christmas.' Naomi's shuffling out the door, dragging cases behind her.

'Yeah, you too. Have a nice time.' Poised on the edge of his seat, Matt listens for the final farewells, for the keys locking the door again. 'Well?' His hand catches Sarah's forearm as she tries to move past.

'Well, what?' Tugging her arm back, Sarah jumps back into her corner, nudging into her collection of pillows. On her lips are the traces of the giggle fit she had before, 'Did you really go to Costa Rica?'

Matt wastes no time in leaping couches, sitting at Sarah's feet, 'Why? Did it sound like a lie?'

'I'm not saying you were lying, just you never mentioned it before.'

His head lies back against the sofa, face turning in profile to look at her, 'There's a lot of things I haven't mentioned yet.' Matt's brows raises, all in effort of making his statement seem as ominous as possible.

'S'pose...'

With some effort, he manages to shift Sarah closer to the edge of the sofa, wedging himself so that he can lie down next to where she sits, curled and curious. 'But I never went to Costa Rica.'

Sarah squirms, doing her best not to slip to the floor, curving her body close to Matt's, reaching an arm across his waist to hold her still. 'So why say that?'

'I lie sometimes.' Matt exposes his teeth in a fox-like grin, 'But it's not like real lying. It's more like...story telling. I wouldn't lie about something that mattered.' His hand reaches up to remove the bobble from her plait, slipping the band round his wrist and letting his fingers undo her hair into waves, 'I've never actually even been abroad.'

'Really?'

'Nopes. Always wanted to, though. Just never really had the chance, I guess.'

Sarah carefully lifts a hand, a fingertip tracing the curve of his eyebrow, 'If you could run away anywhere in the world, where would you go?'

'Australia.' Matt's answer is ready, 'Think about it – sun all the time, barbecues every day, I could take up surfing and give the shrimp I caught to the sun-kissed blonde I'd have in my super expensive condo.'

'Blonde?' Sarah's voice wavers, dark eyes looking at the dark hair wound up in Matt's hand.

'Guess a brunette would do. So long as she looked good enough in roller-skates. Just think of all the pictures I could take in Australia. All my photographs round here turn out so dark.'

In danger of letting the conversation turn dark, Sarah offers a placating smile, finger resting on the tip of his nose, 'I look good in roller-skates.'

'Oh, really?' His eyes go cross for a moment, focusing on her finger, the blur of her pale skin and red nails on his nose, 'Then you should run away with me. What say you?'

Sarah's laughter rolls out warm against his lips, 'I don't know. What's in it for me?'

'Uhm - a surfer boyfriend and you can decorate the house however you like. Scented candles and fairy lights everywhere.'

Her hand moves to her forehead, elbow bent in a salute, 'Aye, aye Captain. Sounds like a good plan to me.'

'Actually, I dunno. I mean, having a girl on board is always bad luck.' Matt's brow creases while he considers the problem, waiting for Sarah's reaction.

'Look, do you want your sun-kissed, roller-skating girlfriend or not?' Her voice rises and strengthens in warning.

Matt presses his grin against Sarah's feigned pout, lips and eyelashes brushing, 'I suppose so.'

FIFTEEN

Sarah

Fat garlands of red and gold tinsel, tangled and twisted from being in boxes all year long. It's only cheap stuff anyway, and in all honesty I'm surprised it even survived the season. Just a little bit of tinsel, some tacky looking window stickers, a few strands of silver beads and the occasional tree decoration. I had spent Christmas at home, and Naomi celebrates Hanukkah, but I must have felt in a good enough mood to warrant a little bit of festive cheer last year.

'Is that everything?' Matt's voice calls down through the ceiling.

'Yeah, that's it.'

His footsteps move above me before bare feet are revealed on the top rung of the ladder, 'Pretty boring loft, Sarah.'

Pulling out the tinsel, concentrating on detangling it from strings of beads, 'I know. Mum said she wanted *everything* out of there before I moved in. She didn't want any ghosts hanging around for their stuff, apparently.'

'That's a shame. Could've been quite fun.' Jeans appear, then a white t-shirt followed by a stubbly jaw with a smile.

'If you ever leave this place, you should hide some really creepy stuff for the next people to find.'

Taking the tinsel into the kitchen, I know I saw the Sellotape somewhere. In the cutlery drawer? 'Shit!' Large knife in my hand, I jump when Matt grabs behind at my waist. I wriggle free and turn beneath his hand, wielding the weapon between the two of us, 'Oh my *God*, Matt. I nearly killed you.'

He's innocent, lifting both hands and showing empty palms, 'I'm stepping away, stepping away. What are you looking for?'

'Sellotape.' Resigned, I throw the kitchen knife back before anyone does get injured, slamming the door shut.

'Okay, which hand?' His hands are balled into fists, arms raised out zombie-like. His head tilts while he waits for me to choose.

Guessing, playing along, I point at his left hand.

He turns it over to reveal nothing,

'Too bad. Try again.' All repeated, but I smile and choose the same hand again. 'Ta da!' The triumphant revealing of the Sellotape.

'Thanks. I'm going to go hang this up.' Dragging the stepladder along the hallway floor to stop in front of the living room. Not always the most steady on my feet, I rip the tape with my teeth first and stick it to the ends of the tinsel *before* climbing the steps.

'Looks nice up there.' Matt takes the tape from my hand, sticking some to the ends of the gold tinsel and moving to hang it above my bedroom door. 'We're almost going to have a proper Christmas.'

'Really? And what exactly is a 'proper' Christmas?' In my memory of twenty two Christmases, I think there may have been one or two that were 'proper'. At seven and eight years old. Two consecutive years of stocking fillers and presents beneath a tree. Dinner with me, Mum and Dad. Just the three of us round the table, Mum in an apron serving food from a caterer. The Queen's speech and episodes of *Only Fools and Horses*. My parents kissing under mistletoe while I cradled whatever the biggest craze was that year. Going to bed feeling full and happy, leaving Mum and Dad to cuddle on the sofa by the fire. A catalogue Christmas, like a John Lewis advert.

'Proper means no arguing, no shouting...no fighting, basically. A propa Chrimbo.' Matt disappears around me, going to turn on the CD player on the bookshelf. He glances at the stack of CDs beside it before deciding to tune into the radio, 'There must be Christmas songs on somewhere.' The static whizzes in and out, songs rising and fading into noise until he pauses at a brass band playing what sounds like a medley of various seasonal themes.

'How do you know there's not going to be any fighting?' I let the question linger in the doorframe before disappearing into the kitchen. The window is steamed up from having the heating on high, the cold evening air black outside.

'Because if it does, then I'll steal your Christmas and you won't have any to complain about.' But he doesn't make a very convincing Grinch, peeling the window stickers apart and separating scary looking snowmen from a drunken-faced Father Christmas. He's busy concentrating on his display, having a string of snowmen hand in hand, with reindeer flying overhead amid various sized glittery snowflakes. He looks at the red and white figure in his hand, contemplating where to place Santa. He ends up standing on top of the biggest snowflake. Standing back to admire his work, he glances at me, seeking my opinion.

'It's lovely. I like the hand in hand snowmen.'

'Like the scene in *The Snowman*, get it? They're having a drunken ceilidh.'

My laughter mingles with the boiling kettle, and I pull out the two biggest mugs I can find. I'm about to ask if he wants some hot chocolate but -

'I like *The Snowman*. Pretty sure I watch it every year. And we can watch it tomorrow; it's always on Christmas Eve.'

He's not objecting when I start spooning out the hot chocolate, 'We will. Don't worry. So long as you watch *It's A Wonderful Life* with me.'

'I'm sure that can be arranged. I've never seen it, but my mum and my sister used to watch it every year together and they'd always cry.'

What do I say now? Concentrating hard to making sure I add just the right amount of milk to the water, enough to make the chocolate fluffy. Matt never mentions his family unless forced to, and now he's offering nostalgic information.

'Well, you can cry on my shoulder if you need to.' An attempt at making light, a joke, but as soon as it's out of my mouth I know that it's failed. At least I've got hot chocolate to make things better. 'Here.' I slide the mug across gently, a peace offering.

'Thanks.' Matt acts as though the subject was never even mentioned, cradling his mug and padding across laminate flooring for a sofa, 'Let's see what repeats are on.'

Matt's lighting some candles on the coffee table, a series of vanilla and apple spice scents. He picks up a red tea light and sniffs at it, his nose almost touching the wick. 'This one smells like Christmas.' Sharing his discovery, he passes it to me and I put my mug down on a coaster before getting cosy on the sofa.

'Mmm... That's the apple and cinnamon one, I think.' It's impossible not to laugh as my statement causes some kind of revelation in Matt and his eyes widen, reaching to take the candle back.

'It's just like the smell when you make mince pies. We *need* to get some mince pies for tomorrow. Enough for us both and for Rudolph.' Smiling like an excited child, bending to light the candle with a match. He doesn't blow out the flame right away, just watches it burn black down to his fingertips. The flame is fizzing orange, but he puts it out with just a flick of his wrist, the grey smoke curling towards the ceiling.

'Do you want to try making our own?' I don't have the slightest clue about how to make mince pies, but I'm sure I have a recipe somewhere in all those cake books I've got. If I can make cupcakes, I'm sure mince pies are manageable. But who cares if they end up shit? Matt's looking at me like I couldn't have possibly suggested anything more amazing. This is how Christmas should feel: cosy, warm, in love and smelling of cinnamon.

He sits up on the sofa, lying back and lifting his feet to rest across my knees. His eyes do a quick search for the remote, and I dig my hands behind my cushion to retrieve it; I'm sure I left it round here somewhere. Found, I turn the TV on before tossing the remote for Matt to catch, which he does, promptly beginning his search for something worth watching.

'I can't wait for mince pies.' His breath catches in his throat, like he's about to say something more. But he doesn't. The pause just rests there between us.

I want to ask him, but don't want to press him, don't want to push subjects that he's not willing to discuss. But then, he'd almost said it. 'What were you going to say?' The question is raised in what I hope is a vaguely interested way, my eyes remaining on an *Eastenders* special, everyone in paper hats. I don't want to scare him away by staring.

'Nah...Just going to say that I used to help my mum make them. Used to get all covered in flour, and I'd steal the marzipan from the Christmas cake.' Matt's also looking at the television, equally as non-interested in the family quarrels on-screen.

There's something about this time of year, something that's making him nostalgic, dragging up memories of a family he's so sure he doesn't care about. He's so sure that they don't care about him. 'You know, you don't have to stay here for Christmas.' As much as it would pain me to spend the day alone, I'm quite sure I would cope. Would be worse to think I was keeping him prisoner.

He nearly tips from the sofa as he reaches for his mug, and my hands hold tightly around his calves, 'Don't worry. I'm not going anywhere. This is much nicer, trust me.' His smile curls from the top of his mug, eyes blinking with sad honesty.

But he's probably just being nice. 'No, really. I mean, you watch The Snowman with your sister, and make mince pies with your mum...'

'Yeah, maybe, when I was 15. It's not been like that at home for years.' He's hiding behind his mug, and I find that I'm hiding behind mine.

'How come?' Trying not to seem a nasty kind of nosey.

Matt's sigh is heavy, and he pulls his legs away to gather himself on the far side of the couch. Opposite ends. He's staring into his mug, looking for some kind of answer, a way to reply.

'I didn't go to Costa Rica. I didn't finish any kind of degree.' His chest heaves with a deep intake of breath, and there's a foreboding sense that something will be revealed, and it's keeping me distant. 'Where I actually was, was...in an institution. For mental patients. A home. Mental health. Because I tried to kill myself. Commit suicide. Several times. They had to keep me in. Y'know, the skin graft and stuff. That's where I was. Not getting clever, not saving turtles, just shuffling around and trying to stay sane.'

There's more to this story, but I don't need to know it right now. I put my mug down so heavily on the floor that the chocolate laps and splashes over the side. Sitting beside him now, as close as possible, my arms tight around his shoulders, my lips pressed to the top of his ear. But for the shaking of his hands, he's entirely still.

My grip around him slackens as he takes another breath, ready to give more.

'My family hated me after that. After the first time, they weren't happy, but at least they tried to help. Second time round, they didn't want to know. Like, they'd given me everything and I was chucking it all away. But I didn't want to. I had to. It's in my brain. Like a worm, crawling around, digging at me all the time. Third time I went to Mum for help. The blood was seriously everywhere. I dripped it all down the stairs. That's when I got the skin graft, and that's when I went in.'

Struggling, struggling to think. Words. I need to say something. But what? I want to tell him that everything is okay, that I'm here, that I promise that I'll make him happy. But I'm sure he's heard it all before; family, friends, pillow talk. All I can do is hold him closer and hope.

'I'm sorry.' Stupid words, but it's all that manages to come out of my mouth.

'Why? It's not your fault.' He places his mug down on the floor, and twists to face me. He's got a smile on his lips, but his eyes are focused, steady.

All I see is blue. Pale blue, flecked with dark blue, spots of black. Turquoise, green, a ring around widening pupils. Staring so long I can feel the colour rising to my cheeks, my ears warming. So I'm looking at his hands instead, watching as his fingertips push against mine. 'I know.' He's offered so much, and all I can think is to agree. No coherent sentences forming in my brain. Nothing useful, nothing...profound.

'But I'm -'

Matt presses a finger to my lips, smiling brightly with his own.

'Sarah, it's over.' His shoulders roll into a half-shrug, 'Okay, so maybe not completely.' And he removes his finger to kiss my lips lightly, and it's impossible not to smile. 'But the worst is done. I'm on medication and stuff. God knows, I've seen enough psychologists. It's working out. I have a job...I have you. Simple, but...'

I don't want to say anything. Just keep him speaking. Just listen to him telling me that everything is okay.

'Guess most people take stuff like jobs and girls for granted but...in that house, that was all I wanted.' Tackled back into the cushions, his arms wriggle round my back, nuzzling into my neck. He's saying something I can't make out, his voice muffled. Giggling, I can't hear anyway, his breath and his stubble tickling as he tries again to speak.

Wriggling away I can sit up, able now to actually breathe, gasping for air while my ribs start to ache. 'But I'm here for you.' Doing my best to slip into seriousness, 'You can talk to me. So, you're not on your own. Any time you need me.'

Matt's better than this than I am. For all that's been said, all that I know, he's holding his expression so carefully. 'I know.'

SIXTEEN

Matt

Daylight, barely there, filters in through the white curtains, threatening to wake the bodies cosied beneath the duvet. Matt stirs, an ankle flexing, toes stretching out into the coolness of morning. Eyes flicker open, met with a view of tangled dark waves. His hand reaches out over a pale shoulder, not his own, and the body twists to face him. Sarah's eyes meet his, still misty with the recollection of dreams, and her smile widens with the realisation of where she really is.

'Merry Christmas.' Soft laughter tumbles into the bedroom as they greet each other at the same time and Matt pulls Sarah closer, trapping her with a triumphant, 'Jinx!'

Head still heavy from mulled wine, Matt struggles to let go and sits up, once again pleased that Sarah's parents can afford to constantly run the central heating. A hand runs back through his hair, tugging at the ends.

'Are you bored?' Sarah shuffles up next to him, drawing up the duvet to cover them both.

Perhaps there's still something niggling in her mind, some kind of doubt about his being there. Regardless,

Matt smiles and shakes his head, and presses a hand against his ear. 'Are you kidding?' He tilts his head to plant a kiss on her cheek, a hand seeking hers in the folds of the duvet, 'I'd be bored if I was back at mine. I mean, who wants to play third wheel on Christmas Day?' Matt shudders, thoughts of Sue in some kind of Ann Summers Santa costume chasing Dan about the flat - it had happened before, so it could happen again. At least the real Father Christmas has fewer wobbly bits.

Sarah stifles a yawn, moving closer still and resting her face on his shoulder. Her head shakes, and she kisses lightly against his shoulder blade. 'You can be first wheel here, if you like.'

'Works for me.' He nods his approval, distracted by wondering how Dan's day was going, 'You know he's planning on proposing to her today.'

'Seriously?' Sarah's peaked and piqued, raising her head like an inquisitive meerkat; highly amused, and expectant of more information.

'Yup. Says he's going to leave it, like her last present or something. And be all, "Ooh look, one more present! Oh gosh!" and then he's going give her the box and she'll open it and it'll be one of those big sweet rings.' He pauses to turn to Sarah, making sure she's listening, 'Know the ones?' Encouraged by a nod he continues, 'Yeah, and she'll be all surprised but disappointed. I don't know. I figure once she sees the little jewellery box she'll just be disappointed and stuff but Dan thinks it's in her sense of humour to laugh and love it. Anyway, after this happens he's going to give her the real actual ring sometime.'

'In the Christmas pudding?' Sarah's perhaps more excited by the story than she should be. It was never intended to be entertaining, but her eyes are bright as she ties her hair back.

Matt rolls his shoulders, bones in his neck cracking, 'Think so. That, or he said something about getting it into a cracker.'

'Aww, really? That's *sweet*.' Too much emphasis on the double 'ee', she's close to melting into some kind of womanly hysterics.

'You think so?' Matt considers this, like considering for the first time that Dan's idea isn't actually disgusting, or plain stupid. 'Don't you think it's kind of...cheesy?'

'Well, yeah, of course it is. But she'll have such a good story to tell everyone, and she'll never forgot it. I met this one girl that said she and her boyfriend just had a conversation one night and decided that marriage would be a good idea. Isn't that sad? Sitting watching TV and just *deciding* that you should get married?'

'That's definitely worse. I mean, if that's what the proposal is like, what the hell's their married life gonna be like? Boring as fuck.'

Having spoken his mind, Matt lapses into silence. What is the difference between Dan and Sue, and himself and Sarah? So his friend has a couple of years on his own relationship. In fact, it's hard to tell when or if whatever's going on could be called a relationship. There were no cringy one liners, no proclamations of love over the phone, in an email, in person or anywhere. Sarah just wasn't there, and then she was.

Right now, she's redoing her ponytail, a silver bobble held lightly between her teeth while her hands rake long dark waves behind her head. Her head tilts, her lips smile and she tries to speak with the plastic in her mouth, 'You okay?'

It doesn't come out perfectly, but he understands, watching her lips rather than hearing her out loud. So he nods in response, his head still muffled from the effects of mulled wine, brain still ticking trying to figure out what's going on, what he's doing here. This relationship, it all came so easily, like Matt and Sarah were supposed to be played out. And finally it is two bare bodies, warm in each other's company beneath shared covers. Sharing Christmas, a memory that won't be erased. What did you do that Christmas? That Christmas was the one where... The one where he's reaching over the bed, digging around a pile of clothes and books for a stocking. A knitted green stocking patterned with red snowflakes.

'Merry Christmas.' He says it again, just for good measure, offering it to Sarah, the corners of wrapped presents poking out between the patchy wool.

'A stocking! Oh my God, Matt. It's been *years* since I've had a stocking!' She pulls the thing towards her with much the same zest as a three year old would, 'Is this for me?'

Matt nods, heart swelling balloon sized to see just how well his surprise is going. Swelling and swelling as she carefully removes the first present, her eyes still wide with childlike excitement. A red nail picks at the tape: she chose the polish because it was festive, she said. And it was, matching the designs on the paper. But the balloon stops filling, pausing as he holds his breath; hoping and hoping she'll like it, and he's close to whispering prayers.

Heavy silence is broken by a pleasant laughter, a fluffy penguin emerging from the wrapping, 'Aww, he's so cute! I love his little bow tie.' Sarah lifts the plush toy in front of her face, raising its little bead eye level with her own. Then she pulls it towards her, planting a generous kiss on the end of its beak, 'I love penguins.' Statement made with fondness, said softly and lingering, almost confused at receiving a gift that genuinely means something.

'I know,' is Matt's reply, because he knows her words are loaded. He's noticed the penguin toys on her windowsill, the little chain that dangles from her mobile phone, the foam mask that hangs from a handle on her wardrobe.

She's just gazing at it now, still holding it aloft like baby Simba on Pride Rock. There's something going on inside her head, something she's really struggling with. 'I'll call you...'

And suddenly it seems that the biggest worry in the world is whether Sarah can think of a name for the penguin. He watches her face, her nose wrinkling in concentration. 'How about...Penguin?' He offers in an attempt to make it easier for her.

But she shoots him a mean look, like he was being stupid, and her eyes focus back on the penguin's little buttons, 'I think...Pedro!'

'Pedro?'

'Pedro.'

'Very exotic name for a penguin, don't you think?' Matt looks at the toy, glad that he chose the one with red bow tie because it looks much nicer than the one with the green. All the same, Pedro does seem too exotic, too hot, for a penguin.

Cuddling Pedro close to her chest, Sarah raises her eyebrows in warning. 'He's a very special gentleman, and he can have any name he likes. And he likes Pedro.' With a hand on the back of where a neck might be, she pushes to make the toy nod.

'Alright, I'm sorry Pedro,' he reaches out a hand and pats lightly on its tufts of hair. Stretching his arm he pokes at the sides of the stocking, still bulging with hidden presents; a gentle reminder.

With another long look at the penguin, Sarah places it carefully between them on the bed, making sure he won't fall over. Then she's reaching into the stocking, fingers closing around the next present. 'You're very good at wrapping presents – I'm impressed.'

And so is Matt, if he's being honest with himself. This wasn't just a case of throwing a mixed CD at a friend, or handing over a bottle of whisky, or throwing a bunch of things into a gift bag. Painstaking labour had gone into choosing the right paper, and then he'd flicked through endless Youtube videos, seeking professional help on gift wrapping. 'Thanks.'

The next present comes out, long and thin. Beneath Matt's wrapping paper, the box is secured with a silver ribbon, all the trimmings that make it seem special. Slipping the ribbon round the corners without undoing the bow, Sarah gently lifts the lid off the box. Her surprise is announced by a soft intake of breath, a string of gold held across both palms. Dusty sunlight flits around the bracelet and gives it an extra sparkle, and Sarah's still staring, shifting to rest it in one hand so that she can touch it with her fingertips.

'I don't really know. It's nice. I mean, it'll really suit you. Your eyes, and your skin. I don't know. It's a charm bracelet.' Matt offers the information in a rush, words that he desperately needs to get out. He squints to survey Sarah's face, not sure if the silence is awe or confusion. Maybe it was a bad idea after all, but the woman in the jewellers assured him, had practically promised that it would be perfect.

Sarah wraps the bracelet around her wrist, holding out her hand for help with the clasp, 'Matt, it's really, really beautiful.' She speaks with deep breaths, like she's weighing her words out carefully, 'And so...thoughtful.'

Matt's fingers fumble with the delicate chain, afraid that if he's not careful the thing will snap. He's suddenly reminded of an image from a picture book; a princess weaving straw into gold.

'Least now I know what to get you every birthday and Christmas.' His laughter is uneasy with the boldness of his statement. There might not be another Christmas like this; she'd surely come to her senses by then. Either way, he knew from the way she examined the little lock and key charms, she wasn't going to throw it away any time soon.

Sarah smiles at his suggestion, pleased with either the sentiment of the present, or the prospect of there being more times like these. There's no space for thinking between them, too busy enjoying a moment of shared happiness. Rare as they are, there's no time for breaking into thoughts or worries. She's digging into the bottom of the stocking now, taking out the remaining couple of presents, laughing at the obligatory orange at the bottom.

But the present opening rituals are lost on Matt, responding to Sarah's reactions without saying another word. He smiles when she smiles, smiles when she laughs, smiles when she wraps him up in a fluffy pink dressing-gown and leads him through to the living room. These moments are too surreal for Matt, and he's struggling to focus. Sarah lets go of Matt's hand, and gestures towards the centre of the room. On the coffee table is a small pile of presents, all wrapped up in green paper. It takes another few seconds and some words from Sarah, before he realises that the gifts are for him. But the realisation kick-starts him back into his Christmas morning, and he turns to Sarah to give her hand a squeeze.

She shouldn't have. Really, she shouldn't. Breakfast in bed would do just fine, maybe an HMV voucher thrown in. But here he was, unwrapping presents that she'd chosen and bought herself. Things she personally thought that he'd like, with money that she'd worked hard for. Sure, it was the same deal when Matt had bought Sarah's presents, but he hadn't considered just how careful and intimate it was to have someone do the same for him. For years any kind of present he'd received had been some description of shot, or bottle, or inflatable sheep. Here and now: a pair of

Batman slippers, the photo frames he wanted, that trilby hat that he'd joked about, and, 'Paintballing?'

Sarah's watching so keenly she's nearly fallen off her perch at the edge of the couch, 'Mhm...you said that you -'

'That I always wanted to go. And you remembered.' Matt looks over the leaflets in his hand, all the details about where to go, what to expect, how many paintballs you get, what to wear...

'And don't worry, you don't have to take me. You can go with Dan, or whoever. Not sure I'll be much of an opponent.' Sarah leans to look at the leaflet, resting her chin on his shoulder to read over it.

'I'm not really sure how much of a fighter I am, in all fairness.' Matt folds the leaflet closed and bundles the various bits of paper together, lifting a hand to rest on top of Sarah's head. They stare, straight ahead, to the switched off television decorated with Christmas cards. From Dan (and Sue), from Laura (with best wishes), from Sarah's Dad (still miss you and love you), and a hastily scribbled effort from the Cairns family that Matt had added to the collection. 'But it sounds like fun.'

Sarah's head tilts and she pecks at Matt's cheek before standing to her feet, 'You've got about a year or something to decide when you want to go so there's no rush.'

Matt stretches luxuriously, arms above his head and legs protruding from the hem of the bathrobe, like he's suddenly growing inside Wonderland clothing. Eventually he struggles to his feet, fumbling to tighten the thick pink tie around his waist.

'Thanks, Sarah.' His voice comes softer than he anticipates, and his cheeks flush pink with embarrassment and the warmth of the room, 'Really thoughtful presents. I appreciate that.' He grabs at Sarah's waist before she can escape to the door, twisting her round to face him. Matt's smile beams his sentiment, every fibre of his being silently trying to communicate just how grateful he is. What can he say? Thank you, thanks so much, I appreciate it, I'm truly grateful. Anyone can say these words, and he's painfully aware that the words he'd use are those that any person would use for any presents. But these are special, they are personal, and it's all he can do but telepathically transfer his thoughts with a kiss.

Seemingly it's worked, and Sarah's heavy in his arms, muttering, 'You're welcome' once and twice and again. Overwhelmed with the moment, she relaxes against his chest, arms reaching around his back to hold him as close as possible.

Too much. It's too much to have Christmas morning, or afternoon, whatever time it happened to be. Hard to have gotten through presents without bitter words, or those dreaded false thanks. He slowly unwraps Sarah's arms from his body, gently removing a limpet from its rock.

Cosy, but he needs to breathe. Something ticks inside, a force that threatens to suffocate. But, detached, she doesn't seem wounded, because Matt's sitting on the sofa, pulling on his new slippers. 'What do you think?' His feet bounce from side to side, Batman logos blurring.

'Very handsome. C'mon, Batman, what's for breakfast?'

Satisfied with the distraction, the compliments, and the excellent black and yellow slippers, Matt stands to attention before sashaying Sarah through to the kitchen.

'Madam, take a seat, make yourself comfortable, and be ready for the most spectacular display of cooking you have ever experienced.'

SEVENTEEN

Matt

On fire. Electric. Liquid. Breezing onto the dance floor, every element of a party. Why shouldn't they join in? The world is their oyster too. Breaking it open in the middle of a dance floor, just minutes before a new year. A new start. Everything changes on the first of January. Brighter, fresher. The moment is drawing closer, the crowd huddles together in anticipation of something great. Resolutions ready to be made. This year they will be happy, this year they will take on the world.

Music stops. Collective breath held before the DJ calls out, 'TEN!' And the countdown continues, holding hands, holding gazes, calling out the numbers like declarations of love.

'THREE!' They pull closer.

'TWO!' Fingers clutching.

'ONE!' The room breaks into applause, cheers, the words 'new year' and 'Hogmanay' yelled out with triumph. Matt and Sarah welcome each other into promises, whispering together, 'Happy New Year.' They pull apart, if only to kiss. This is what 2010 will feel like; just bliss, just each other.

The room shifts around them and they are separated by strange hands, becoming part of a circle of many across the dance floor. Holding hands with people they don't know, people they don't see, just laughing at the situation as the words of Auld Lang Syne roll automatically from their lips. That's just how life is: absurd and amusing, warm and buzzing.

Matt rolls up his sleeves, ready to face his world. White scars flash silver beneath disco lights, ultra violet rays illuminate smiling teeth. He's still got it, and he knows it. Hard to ignore with Sarah's arms wrapped about his neck, hip bones pressed together. Whispers exchange and they head for the bar, joining a hustle and bustle of sweating bodies. Everyone is happy to stand back, let others go first. 2010 and people remember their manners.

'Happy New Year!' and there is something so genuinely happy about Matt's greeting to the bar man that the words are infectious, spreading along the bar and roaring from the waiting crowd.

'Happy New Year, mate. What're you after?' Rubbing the sweat from his hair on the thighs of his jeans, trying not to show disappointment at working while everyone else plays.

'Eh...two JD and cokes, please.' Picking at coins in his wallet, trying to figure out which is worth anything, mistaking five pences for pound coins. Exchange over,

Matt and Sarah give smiles of gratitude before finding a space to lean with their drinks. They casually survey the scene, eyeing beating bodies while they sip from the glass. Waiting is fine, catching a breather. Neither of them like this song anyway, simultaneously raising eyebrows while groups writhe around to a steady rhythm.

Sarah finishes hers just before Matt and she takes a quick lunge forward to put her empty glass on a shelf, out of the way of feet. Simultaneously, a figure charges past apparently from nowhere, dashing through the lasers from the smoke clouds. Sarah aims to move away as quickly as possible, hand raised as an apology sits ready on her tongue. But the stranger gets there first, voice gruff and heavy.

'Fucking freak.'

She's slow to react to the brute of a man, bald head reflecting the mirrored light of the disco ball. Matt's directly behind her, a protective arm held across her chest.

'What's that?' Sarah can't see his face but she can feel his muscles tensing around her, notes the heavy rise and fall of his chest against her back.

'Fuck-ing freak.' The words are repeated heavily, the man's breath stinking of booze, his sweat reeking of marijuana. 'You fucking fick?' His eyes are hidden beneath thick eyebrows, but Sarah tenses as he sizes her up, 'Don't you even feed yer bird?'

Sarah: a stone lighter than months before, new clothes of a smaller size, slim calves and no stomach. She lifts a shaking hand, pressing fingers into Matt's arm; keeping him close, holding him back.

His voice whispers forward from between clenched teeth. 'Just leave her out of this.' The panic softens as Matt's arm moves to hook Sarah's elbow, tugging at her gently.

'Couple of freaks, ain't they?'

He's joined by a bigger friend, scratching at a bush of black beard flecked with beer foam. 'Whassat?'

'This skinny lass and her queer boyfriend.' Matt has already stepped away, keeping his eyes trained on the men, careful not to turn his back. 'Cut yourself cause no one understands?' His voice booms across the quiet between songs.

Glass.

Smash.

'You fucking -'

'Don't you ever!'

Thud.

Screams.

'Stop! Stop!'

'Enough. *Enough.*' Scrambling, a wall of a bouncer pulling the two apart, warning off the crowds that had gathered to watch or 'help out'.

Sarah trots after, the entourage, like she's following the schoolmaster dragging a pair of bullies leaving the other's ear bleeding.

Outside the air is numbing, the cold and empty atmosphere of a year just beginning. Nothing's happened yet. But it has. A kiss and a fight: welcome to 2010. Matt has barely had time to register his surroundings and he's pulling at Sarah, dragging her along as fast as he can without toppling her from her stiletto heels onto the crystallising snow.

'Matt!' Calling him like he's miles away, ignoring taunts and cheers from Cowgate well-wishers. She's hastily pulling the sleeves of her coat over bare arms and shoulders, clutching Matt's jacket to her chest.

Tripping across holes in the cobbled road, Matt pauses to let her catch up. She does, almost leaping up onto the pavement. He says nothing, turning and twisting and running his hands through his hair, pulling at the ends. A siren sounds and his blue eyes widen in panic.

'I didn't mean it.'

'C'mon.'

Now Sarah's in the lead, hiking up the hill with Matt in tow. Somehow it comes across both their minds that he's crazy. Plead insanity, if need be. And it seems like it doesn't matter. They pause against Greyfriar's Bobby, waiting for the adrenaline to pass. Expecting to burst into laughter, perhaps, but not this time. This is too much.

'Let's go home.' Offering smiles and encouraging tones while Matt rolls down the sleeves of his t-shirt.

He doesn't move.

'Are you okay?' Sarah circles him, searching for any sign of injury. Spatterings of blood across his stomach; his or -? She reaches out a hand, as though by touching it she'd know.

'I'm fine.' Matt's reply is too quick, the words clipping the air as he sidesteps around her.

Sarah only catches up with him because he pauses at the kerb to let a rickshaw pass. How the boy will pull that woman up a hill is anyone's guess.

'Where are you going?' Her voice squeaks, feebly offering his jacket.

'Park.' He grabs it from her, feet crunching against gravel on the road. Hippies are collected outside the Forest Café, all faux fur, bandanas and dreadlocks. The crowd parts; the sight of blood makes people nervous – either someone's been hurt, or someone's been doing the hurting. Shouts of what the fuck. Screams of ambulance and police - better to keep safe, in case of the latter. He's quick to fasten the buttons of his coat, hiding evidence of a fight.

The smoking and chatting resume, some still watching Matt's back as he ignores the rules of the red man. Nobody parts for Sarah: just a girl tottering across the ice, using inches of heel as a pick axe to keep her steady. Various conversations reach her as she tiptoes around the group, lifting her eyes from the snow for a moment to catch sight of Matt hurrying through the square.

He pauses by the union, loud and lit up with strings of lanterns and real flame torches. Heavy ceilidh sounds and laughter drift through open windows. Where's Sarah? Panic sets in, but she slides round the corner, arms flailing like broken sails.

'Hey,' Matt wraps an arm around her waist, 'Let's go home.'

Steadied by his side, Sarah walks in silence, grateful when they reach the grass of the Meadows. Digging her heels into the hard soil, she pauses. Waiting for action, an order; waiting for more words.

Matt's reaching for the same, averting his gaze while he comes up with something, anything. The thoughts are forming foggily in his mind when the first snowflakes fall, tiny drops like rain. 'It's snowing.'

Sarah lifts her face as they fall in a flurry and her kiss lands warm on Matt's lips, showing her appreciation of the weather as though he had made it so.

'So we can start again, right? The snow as a blanket over the blood of the fight, right? Just an early new year hiccup.'

Sarah nods, glad at least he's admitted that it actually happened. The word 'fight' means anger and violence, but there was no guarantee that Matt had associated himself with those words. A fight was a fight, it was over, and he wanted it gone. Surely that was good enough.

'I fucking love snow!' The half-buttoned coat is off as quickly as it was on, tossed aside as the goose pimples rise instantly along his arms.

'Me too!' Too warm to lose her own jacket, Sarah is content in spreading her arms, palms open to the sky, catching flakes in her red hands.

Now Matt's at her knees, raw fingers digging through snow and ice, grass and dirt clumping at the tips of his nails. The t-shirt is removed, flung into the space between his knees, and he's covering it up, scooping snow over the persisting crimson colour, intent on giving the thing a good burial. As he stretches to stand, his boots press down over the pile just to be sure that the thing doesn't and can't come back. The orange glow from a flickering street lamp reveals fresh scratches along his shoulder, red etchings made into his shoulder blade.

'There.' It is finished, and Matt tips back his head, extending his tongue to savour the snowy downpour. He's clutching at Sarah, letting her taste the wet chill in his mouth, her tongue searching for warmth.

Sarah watches, head tilted and dipped, as Matt picks up his coat, beating it against his thigh to get rid of the crusts of snow.

He laughs at her expression, following the tract of her gaze to the small mound of earth and ice between them, 'No one will ever know.' He takes Sarah's hand, pulls her close, nuzzling his nose into the warm space between the collar of her coat and her neck.

Resisting but reluctant, Sarah wriggles free of Matt's tightening embrace, raising a hand and rubbing it at the end of her nose. Brown eyes are lost as they search Matt over, looking for something that felt missing. A spot the difference game; there was more change than just a shirt beneath the snow.

'I'm cold,' is all she says.

Matt takes her hand again, this time placing it in his pocket. Together again, side by side. He wipes his own hand against his jeans, drying it before wrapping it around Sarah's tiny icy fingers. There's no getting away this time.

And they're content just to be; happy to be standing, then walking, tracing over hundreds of disappearing footsteps imprinted on the pavements. In the opposite direction, retreating from the masses, from crowds, from others. Seeking out warmth, each other, comfort of some sort.

'At least no one can bother us at home,' is all he says.

EIGHTEEN

Sarah

His phone should be vibrating in his pocket, it should be bleeping to remind him. Ten, twelve missed calls? So he's not a reliable texter and most of the time I shouldn't expect a reply. One hour twenty five minutes and nothing. Landline. He wrote it down somewhere, he said, 'Just in case.' The desk drawer is full of bills, scraps of paper, letters with official stamps and headings - information impossible to throw away, just in case. An unassuming envelope, *Sarah* scribbled in a mannish scrawl, the tail on the 'S' unnecessarily long. This letter is a couple of months old now, the coloured ink still bright.

One day early December when Matt was amused by my collection of stationery; gel pens in every colour, glittery ones and scented ones too. Paper edged with fairies and flowers, the occasional cute woodland critter. I write to no one, but Matt wrote to me. On my return from the shower I found the letter on my pillow, Matt gazing triumphantly as he cleaned smudged pink stains from his fingers with a face wipe.

Dear Sarah,

I am writing you a letter. Isn't that profound? Like Darcy to his ~~Jane Eyre~~ Elizabeth. Now you have no excuse not to keep in touch with me forever (unless you burn this or bin it, obviously).

An address. Two phone numbers.

'Hello?' A very vaguely familiar voice.

'Uhm, hi, it's Sarah. Is Matt in?'

'No, sorry. Do you want me to -'

The face swims into view behind my closed eyes. It's just Sue; nothing to be worried about. 'Do you know where he is?'

'Forth Road Bridge. He went -'

'Okaythanksbye.'

Forth Road Bridge. Forth Road Bridge.

Grey, height, river, newspaper, headlines. All these come to mind at the sounds of the words. They've come to sound quite ominous.

My fingers slide over the screen of the phone, flipping through endless unnecessary applications. Wipe my hands on my jeans and start again. 'Lisa, Lisa, are you up?'

'I am now.' Groggy, hungover tones and stifled male laughter.

'You're hungover.' Stating the obvious.

'Well, duh, Sarah.' And she knows so too.

'So you can't drive?'

Lisa's throat gurgles in the negative, 'I can barely see. I'm not going anywhere.'

Shit.

'Alright, well, thanks anyway.' Stringing words out from between clenched teeth, doing my best at sounding bright, polite. But the buzz that follows hanging up sounds cruel.

How the fuck does anyone get to the bridge? Car. But - Taxi. I really need to tidy out my purse, cursing a collection of receipts, bus tickets, Boots vouchers. Taxi card. Not sure I can hear myself making the call, but my breath rushes over the words. 'As soon as possible.'

Ten minutes is a long time. It takes just one to throw my boots on, my jacket, this faithful handbag is always at the ready to pick up and take. I dig hard at the orange colour on my nails but it doesn't budge. Attempting to occupy myself flaking varnish that is just too fucking expensive to chip.

Bzzz.

Readily startled, racing to the door, nearly forgetting to grab my keys. Tripping down the staircase, bursting through the door, 'Taxi for Clarke.'

'Aye.'

'Forth Road Bridge, please?'

'Whit?' Twisting, incredulous in his driver's seat. 'Forth Road -'

'Yes, please.'

He doesn't even try to hide his disgruntled noises or looks, glancing at me in the rearview mirror as he pulls away.

I hate taxis. Always so awkward, like the driver expects some kind of conversation for his service, like we owe it to each other to banter. Fuck it, he's getting paid, and it'll be a lot by the time this journey's through. It's his job. He will drive me and that's that.

Fortunately, it's looking like he's far from interested, preferring the company of a friendly morning radio voice. Thank God, thank Boogie.

The Edinburgh morning moves too slowly, full of traffic reluctant to reach work. *Sorry, stuck in traffic.*

But I wonder how many of these people are feeling any remorse for delaying the start of their shift. Either way, couldn't care less - somewhere to go, somewhere to be, and Haymarket feels like it lasts forever.

January mornings are synonymous with twilight - a no man's land between sleeping and waking. I'm a stranger here, bright eyed on the hunt, on a mission. Rescuing, but it's taking so long. Red numbers are clocking up money, yellow digits are clocking up time. But I'm going nowhere fast.

Matt

They say that the second your feet leave the edge is when the regret hits. Actually, on second thoughts, it was a bad idea. But there's no time for second thoughts. No last minute check-in to A&E, no stemming a flow of blood, no cutting the cords of a noose. Wham, bam, thank you ma'am. You hit the surface, the waves break your limbs, but you don't feel the water filling your gasping lungs because you're already dead. Irreversible damage.

How many bodies lie beneath the River Forth? How many crabs make homes of skulls, playgrounds of ribcages? Water darkened by sewage and death, a collection of Scotland's waste. Small boats make picturesque the scene, defiant of threatening skies. Matt's just a small speck in his surroundings but he doesn't go unnoticed by many passing vehicles. Collective breath held: is he going to? - surely, not - oh, my God - what a retard out in this weather.

All these voices are shelled, thoughts spoken by people unseen. He can't see them, so they can't see him. Matt has found a place where he can't be pestered by the world, sequestered from the worries of others. X feet above the water, Matt is.

A figure approaches, huddled against wind and a fear of falling. Her feet stamp determinedly, although the noise of her footfall is lost beside the rattle of traffic. Matt doesn't see her, busy gazing through a settling mist. Something inside him causes him to turn, and he watches Sarah come closer. She's dangerously close, cheeks red from weather and emotional exhaustion, the curls of her fringe sticking to her forehead. But she's got a long way to go as he continues to watch her progress through a telescopic lens. To better judge the distance, he lets the camera rest on its strap about his neck. His surprised smile falters as he registers her resolute expression: he had imagined the fierceness to come from her climb, not as the result of emotional exasperation.

'Sarah, what are you doing here?' Pleased nonetheless to find her in a landscape that doesn't match; an exotic bird.

'What am *I* doing here? What am *I* -?' She swallows the salt-air in gulps, her voice reaching the levels of the angry motor vehicles. 'Matt...' This engine stutters and falters, stalled as her gaze flickers to the equipment against Matt's chest.

The air shifts between them, an almost visible change in temperature. Both faces redden, her brown eyes large almonds, his blue eyes small splinters. Sarah's lips part, Matt's lips twist, but neither can offer words.

'I -'

'You -'

The accused and the accuser are in danger of blurring into the background if neither moves. Matt's footstep resonates heavily as his boot presses forward and the next falls in line, a strong but awkward shuffle. There's no attempt to prevent contact, Matt's stooped shoulder colliding lightly with Sarah's jaw.

'Matt. Matt wait - Where...?'

'Going home.' Retracing the steps he'd made an hour before, retracing the fresh ones she'd made.

She says nothing, but trails behind, glancing around like there might be some other way out. Don't look down.

'What did you think was going to happen?' Not daring to look for her answer, tugging sharply at the zip of his camera bag. Impatient, despite waiting for her at the end of the bridge.

'I just wanted to - I was worried.' Explaining nothing exactly, but hopeful it will suffice.

'Matt at the Forth Road Bridge equals disaster, that it?' His brow creases as he dips in to his own thought process, 'How the fuck did you know where I was anyway? Where the hell did you come from?'

'I called your flat. Sue told me.' Eyes trained to his boots, narrowly missing a pile of shit to his left.

'And what? What did she say?'

'Well, I was worried. I - hung up.'

'Let me guess. She said, "Forth Road Bridge" and you thought, "How high?"' Arms akimbo, the fingers of one hand flexing into a fist. In the silence he takes his phone from his pocket, injecting a saccharine boost into his voice,

'Hi mate. Yeah, that's me done. Sure, that's fine. Sarah's here too, by the way. Alright, see ya in a bit boyo.'

He's already walking away, 'Dan's gonna meet us round here and take us home.' Silence for two more streets. Matt holds out a palm to test for rain and, sure of a downfall, lifts his hood. Sarah slips her ever-ready umbrella from her bag, losing herself beneath a dome of white and blue stars. Shuffling closely behind, like a sorry servant after her master.

Beep. Beep.

Dan's arm stretches out of the open window, hand ushering them forward, 'Hurry up! It's gunna pish it down!'

Matt slings the camera carefully from his shoulder, cradling the bag as he slips into the passenger seat. Without invitation from Matt, Sarah pulls down her umbrella and makes vain attempts to shake rain off it. In the back seat the final click of the car door means comfort, if not relief.

'Alright, Sarah? What you doing here?'

'Oh, Sue told me Matt was here and I just wanted to surprise him.' Feeble excuses met with a polite smile in the mirror.

'Get anything good, then?' Hand resting on the gearstick, Dan leans to peek at the camera. Sarah stretches forward, but Matt's hand is cupping the screen.

'Yeah. Some great shots. Thank God I missed the rain though.'

'Know, eh?'

'How're your folks?' Matt stores the SLR camera back safely before clipping in the seat belt.

'Aye, alright. Surprised to see me for brekkie but was good, aye.'

The car pulls out to join a queue at a red light, mother and pram dashing across. During the wait, no one says a word, each glancing out of his or her own window, scrabbling for something to say that might be of remote interest or amusement.

'So, do your parents live here? Is this where you're from, Dan?' Polite ventures from the back seat. She needs to say anything to break the tension, staring into the rear-view mirror in the hopes of catching Matt's eye. But he's busy, finger scrolling round and round on Dan's iPod. Her question is broken as Matt mumbles his own question, dabbing at the thing with a fat finger.

But she's met with niceties from Dan, head nodding as he changes lanes. 'Yeah. My childhood home. Parents have lived here since forever, basically.'

Her voice drifts, a reaction to potentially anything, 'That's nice.'

'What you two up to for the rest of the day? Fancy lunch and a film or something? I'll bring Sue, eh?'

Matt settles on a track; Scottish accents, guitars and noise. 'Sounds good, but I've got...stuff to do.'

NINETEEN

Sarah

'You have no idea, do you? I mean, really, no idea.' Matt's arms are folded as he stands by the door of my bedroom, like he doesn't know if he should stay or go. There's obviously more he needs to say. 'Did you seriously, honestly, think I was going out there to jump?' His stare is overpowering because he's trying to draw a certain answer from me.

The question gets stuck in my brain, whirring round and round while I try to pluck at a reasonable reply. Of course, something burrowed in the recesses of my heart and the pit of my stomach told me at the time that I was being ridiculous. But that stupid head of mine overruled, warning me of logical danger. 'You said your new pills were making you feel funny...' Because in the end that is what had made sense.

'Funny, as in seeing shit and nightmares, not I-want-to-kill-myself funny.' He's accusing me of something, arms held out before him in exasperation. He's either too hot, or he's resigned himself to staying, stepping into the room and dropping his camera bag carefully on my pillow before removing his coat. The camera rolls and lands between the padded feet of Pedro the Penguin and, instinctively, I reach out to clutch it to my chest.

But it doesn't comfort me as much as I hoped, and I put all my attention on the little bow tie. I need to focus on something, collect my thoughts, gather my senses - all the clichés make sense. 'I'm sorry.'

'Do you even know what you're sorry for?' Matt's not angry, just *disappointed.*

They seem like the right words, that an apology is due. But I tried to save his life, not spoil his day. 'I'm...not really sure what you want me to say. I'm sorry that I thought - that I jumped to stupid conclusions.' Shoulders slumping, I feel ready to just slip off the bed and I wriggle my toes to make sure they're still touching floor.

'Sarah...' I know he's been watching me the entire time I've had my head bowed. I know that if I were to turn to look at him, his big blue eyes would be sad and searching and they'd look straight through mine and into my soul. Matt can *do* that. The bed dips as he sits next to me, but I only manage to look at the part of his thigh that lies alongside mine.

'Look, I get what you were trying to do. But you really have to trust me. I mean, it's almost like you were accusing me of cheating or something. Well, not that. But it's like...I feel betrayed somehow.'

My body twitches, physically flinching at the accusation,

but Matt's hand finds my shoulder, moving upwards, gently pressing to rest my head on his shoulder.

'You need to know that I'm not going anywhere. If I'm at the Forth Road Bridge, or at the gun and razor shop.' The vaguest hint of a smile is detectable at his attempt to make things light. He exhales, relaxing as he lays a hand over mine, so I let go of Pedro and he tumbles to the floor. 'What doesn't kill you makes you stronger, and all that, ya know? So... I'm here.' His fingers wrap tightly around mine, like he's making a tangible reality that is clear to both of us.

My heart feels too heavy; it's too intense. So I seek a distraction, reaching over to touch at the zip on the black case.

'Can I see the pictures?'

Matt's only too happy to share his work, and while he sets up the camera I kick off my boots before sitting cross-legged on the bed.

'Yup, here we go.' Matt pulls his legs up, shuffling next to me and we lean against the wall, heads pressed together to see the results.

I know nothing about photography. I don't understand lenses, or lighting, or the differences between cameras. Matt tries to tell me, to show me, so that I can get as giddy about taking pictures as he is. That's not possible, but it wouldn't hurt to know a little. What I do know is the difference between a picture that I love and one I couldn't care less about. As Matt skips slowly through his photographs, I definitely know that these are beautiful. He stops, lifts the screen closer to his eye, then presses buttons to zoom in on things - an area of cloud or a patch of sea. He shakes his head, deletes the image, then continues with the slide show, smiling away as he pleases even himself. Somehow he's capable of making the same scene feel a variety of ways. The familiar view from the bridge shifts from ominous to peaceful, from dirty to glorious. He's lost in his camera, spending longer looking at an image than I need to. So I look at Matt instead and I can't help but warm to that satisfied and humble smile, to his hood-tousled hair. From the way his ankles flex to the tag poking out slightly at the back of his neck. Careful not to wake him, my fingers reach out to tuck the label back in, the motion causing his body to ripple in a shiver.

He turns to me, looks at me, and it's significant because it's the first time our eyes have met since the scene on the bridge. Hello blue, I'm brown.

'So do you like them?' Anxiously asked, like I might have an opinion that actually matters.

'You know, I seriously think you ought to do a display, an exhibit or something.'

Matt's expression melts at the dreamy notion, no doubt accompanying the idea with various vivid images in his mind.

'Why don't you do one at the bar?'

'Huh?' Startled by the prospect of the possible fruition of his dream.

'Well, why not? I mean, Chris is always saying that it's pretty dead during the day, so why not do that? And, maybe you could do it weekly. Bring in bands, or arts and crafts.'

'That, my little genius, sounds *amazing*.'

I nod, flushed at the way his words can hold so much emotion. 'And then you get rich and famous and open up your own photography shop. You can hold workshops there for students. Some people will spend a fortune on that kind of thing.'

'Yes! And you can be my sexy secretary, so I can get some in my tea breaks.'

We're both laughing and I hold up a hand.

'Now slow down, Cairns. *I* will be too busy working in my florist shop, which will be right next to your photo shop.'

'Okay, that's fair enough. But we can still have tea breaks together, yeah?' My assent is murmured through the kiss he's pressing on my lips. 'And we'll get married and call it "Cairns Creative."'

'Ooh. And where will we live?'

'We'll get one of those hu-uge houses on the Grange, surrounded by trees so no one can look in.'

'With a dark room?'

'Naturally. I wouldn't live without one.'

'And a big delicious garden, with cherry blossoms trees and rose bushes and one of those outdoor swings.'

'Anything for Mrs Sarah Cairns Creative.'

The sound of his name next to mine makes me giggle and it bubbles in my stomach until it turns into full laughter. It's not such a bad idea after all; a future of cookies and cuteness that seems entirely plausible. Why shouldn't we get what we what? God knows, we both deserve it.

'But it'll need to be a seriously huge house, cause we're gonna have four kids.'

'Four?' I can feel my eyes widen, 'What do you think I'm made of?'

'Well, you didn't like being an only child, did you?'

My head shakes slowly.

'Exactly. And two isn't enough, and if there's three then there's one in the middle, so four is perfect.'

'Perfect it is then.'

'Good. I'm glad we got that settled. Because perfect doesn't happen overnight, you know, so we'd better get started.'

TWENTY

Matt

'I'm not just some sad story to be pitied.'

Matt watches Sarah from the other side of the bed, assessing her hunched body; a frightened hyena ready to leap. 'But that's not what it's about. It's about talking stuff through, figuring out what's going on inside your head.'

'But I do that with *you*. Why bring someone else into this?' Her eyes widen, pupils morphing as she focuses on the flickering bulb above them.

'Yeah, we do it cause that's what couples do. We need to trust each other. I get that. But I'm not qualified in doing anything with your memories. All I can do is give you cuddles and tell you that it's going to be okay.'

'That's all I need.' Her limbs fold out from her body, stretching languidly across the duvet.

There's a startling honesty in her words, in the way they were breathed. Her statement lingers, dissolving into the bedroom before Matt seems to hear them.

'Is it? I mean, there's only so much I can do. What if an unlimited supply of TLC isn't enough?' He's taking her opinions seriously, weighing the differences occurring in his heart and his head.

'If it's unlimited, it'll always be enough.' There's a finality in her tone as she snakes across to Matt, arms reaching for his promised hugs.

Enough is enough, sometimes. In a sigh Matt relents, holding her close around her shoulders while a hand walks slowly up her leg. A fingertip reaches a bruise and with a frown he draws his hand away.

Sarah pulls back momentarily, seeking the cause for his concern and her own frown appears as she tries to recall how the bruise got there.

'I must have walked into the desk at work or something. It happens a lot.' More than likely.

Satisfied with her answer, Matt turns to face her, resting his lips against her forehead without pressing a kiss.

'See? You make everything better.' She whispers into his shoulder blade but Matt struggles under the sentiment and loosens his embrace.

'I don't, though. Not forever. So long as I'm here and you're there everything is great. But the moment we leave the bedroom everything goes to shit again. There are people out there and all sorts of bullshit going on. That's why you need to talk to someone, and that's why I'm on meds: we can't do it on our own.'

'We? Why we?' Sarah's arms are immediately withdrawn and she gathers her legs to rest beneath her, 'I've managed perfectly fine all my life. It's only been going and doing something about it that makes it all seem weird. It was never an issue 'til Carol started asking me questions.'

Laughter isn't the best response, but while there's nothing funny Matt is amused enough to scoff, 'Managed fine? Yeah, right, Sarah. You've been messed up all your life. You can't call anorexia "managing fine".'

Choking sounds are all she makes, unable to articulate the rush of anger, so Matt's free to continue, 'Your self-esteem is so ridiculously low that you can't even get dressed in the mornings without having a breakdown. You've got at least two mirrors in your bag so that you can always check what you look like. And the pile of make-up you own is ridiculous.' His eyes focus on the chest of drawers by Sarah's desk. He knows that each drawer is filled with eyeshadows and nail paints and a plethora of tinted moisturisers, each product sorted by colour and shade. The desk that, he assumes, was once covered in history textbooks is now bowing under cosmetic mirrors with lights, brushes and bottles of perfume.

'Is this supposed to be funny? What the fuck are you even doing? Like you've got any right to tell me what's wrong. Mr Suicide Attempt. Mr I've-Been-On-So-Many-Different-Meds-But-None-Of-Them-Work. Mr I've-Estranged-My-Family-Cause-I'm-A-Fuck-Up.'

Matt's pulling on jeans, failing to find socks and fumbling with the laces of his shoes. He's grabbing a t-shirt, reaching past Sarah to grab his jumper. Avoiding all eye contact. Crossing the room to grab at his coat, but he's interrupted in reaching the door.

In a vest top and pant shorts, Sarah trembles in the door frame, star shaped as she blocks the exit. 'Where do you think you're going? You're not leaving.'

'Fuck's sake, Sarah.' Any more and he might implode, loaded with anger and wounding words.

'Fuck's sake what, Matt?' Trying to find his face, there and gone as the bulb continues to flicker above his head.

'It's not a fucking competition, you know. I'm not counting scars.'

'What...?' Confused, her limbs soften in the doorframe.

'You're always taking the piss. Like I'm not allowed to be depressed and it's all my fault. So you had a shitty upbringing and you've been through a lot. So what if my childhood was fucking great? So what if I don't have any one to blame? I'm not taking the meds for fun, Sarah. I don't cut because it's fucking funny.'

'But I'm not -'

Matt paces backwards, reaching the dressing table and sinking into the chair. His coat is discarded at his feet, and he swivels the seat around so he's facing the corner of room - a space dedicated to a bookcase of achievements; dance trophies, high school awards, newspaper clippings mounted on card, a degree certificate.

'I don't know where it comes from, and I don't know how it happens, but I can promise you that you have no idea about the shit that goes on inside my head.'

Sarah takes the suggestion like it's somehow not fair.

'But you know how bad I feel some days. You know what I've done myself. I know how you feel.'

'You do *not* fucking know how I feel. No cunt knows how I feel.' Matt's fist slams hard into the edge of the desk, wincing. Perfume bottles shake, a couple fall and a heavy scent of musk and flowers leaks into the space between them.

'Then...tell me. How *do* you feel?' Matt can't place her voice; she's lost somewhere in the scents and the light. But she's there. At least she's still there.

Matt shifts slightly on the chair, facing yet another bookcase, this one small and wide. Sarah's collection of books consists of large history volumes, each title boasting change or revolution. Her paperbacks are pretty; all colourful spines and whimsical titles from a 3 for 2. Matt's own book, the one he'd loaned to her, looks dark and uncomfortable. The pages are yellowing, dog-eared and marked with bus tickets and receipts. 'Have you even read this yet?' He holds the book above his head so that she can see the cover and title, his fingers feeling along the various creases in the spine. Silence answers. 'Read it.'

Spinning round on the chair, Matt looks for Sarah, finding her still in the doorframe, still frightened with her arms outstretched. He makes a show of throwing the book to be sure that she knows she's to catch it.

She does, just, bending to grab it before it hits the floor. She shows vague interested in the thing, eyes scanning over the blurb as somehow who only half knows what it's about.

'The Nightmare Box. Find the story called "The Nightmare Box". It's marked with a postcard.' Page 210 and a picture of the Eiffel Tour with a hurried note from Johnny. Her chest tightens as she reads the words "night", "disappeared" and "cut" with guilt, fear, or both. Unable to continue, not while standing, not with Matt watching. Sarah presses the book closed.

'That box, whatever's in there, that's what goes on in my head.'

TWENTY-ONE

Sarah

Faint piano notes drift from an old radio hidden behind a floral curtain. Scenes of ocean waves, beaches coloured in blue and white. Water bubbles from a fountain in the middle of the table: if it's supposed to soothe it's not working, the optic colours switching from garish red to green to blue. The waiting room is claustrophobic, though I'm the only one in here. Reading literature varies from leaflets about reducing stigma to offers of hardship help and little booklets with emergency numbers. But I'd rather ignore the reasons I'm here, ignore all the reasons why anyone would be here. The door opens and I sit upright, but it's not for me. Another patient, and I'm sure I've seen her somewhere before. We glance at each other, recognising but pretending that we don't. We don't want to share why we're here, and we don't need to know each other's burdens. I pull my phone from my bag, struggling to make anything work with shaky, sweaty fingers. Suddenly engrossed in what I'm doing, like there's something very important in deleting those messages. Do we need milk? What time 2 meet? Cya later lol xx

'Sarah Clarke?' Frail and at least fifty, her eyes are watery green as they look at me expectantly. Gathering my stuff together, I'm sure I'm going to drop something, jacket sleeve trailing across the carpet. She let's me pass through the door before her, motioning to a large armchair at the other side of the room, 'Take a seat.' Her voice is soft but old, like she's used it too much; crackling like paper.

Throwing myself into the seat, I allow myself to sink while I busy myself folding my jacket, putting my phone away. Stalling time.

'Hello, Sarah. My name's Carol, and I'll be your counsellor for the next few weeks. We'll do the initial chats, and then we'll decide where to go from there, okay?' She looks comfortable in her chair, moulded by years of talk and tears. Between us is a small wooden table with flowers, a clock and a box of tissues. How hard can this be?

'Hello.' That's as much as I can manage because I'm panicking. I'm here now. I've ticked the boxes, I've passed the initial interview (well done, you're depressed enough to join), but what next?

'Now, what would you like to talk about? Why did you decide to begin counselling?'

'Well, it was Matt's idea. My boyfriend. He thought that I should talk to someone else, someone that isn't him.' She nods, and it's nerve-wracking. This whole thing, this whole place. This woman, this Carol, staring at me with a pen poised over a yellow pad. Deep breath.

'Because, basically... I'm not really happy. I feel...' What? What do I feel? Mind and heart are at a blank, and I'm trying to remember the conversation I had with Matt last night - all the things that I was going to talk about. 'Messed up. I mean, first there's my family who have messed me up, and messed up their own lives. And I used to have an eating disorder, and sometimes I think about cutting myself but I just don't have the guts to do it and I feel completely lost like I don't know what happens next.'

Carol smiles, encouraging, but she's seen and heard it all before. There's nothing I can bring up in her little office that she doesn't have a response for.

'So let's start with your family. How is your relationship with them?'

'Well, I don't have any brothers or sisters. Just me, Mum and Dad. They just got divorced. Mum's basically an alcoholic. But that's cool, in her friendship group. Everyone's drinking something or prescribed to some kind of drug. And they all have the money to pay for it, somehow. I don't even know where the money comes from.' An awkward giggle escapes, and I feel the desperate need to lighten the leaden tension in the room.

'And Dad, well, he worked somewhere doing something and he always tried to help Mum but she said she didn't need help. And she was obviously sleeping with other men and I guess that upset Dad. Makes sense. Now Dad's with some young American guy in Hawaii or something like that and Mum's just spending money on ridiculous clothes.'

'And how do you think that has affected you?'

'It left me really lonely. I was always with a different *au pair*, or nanny or maid or whatever. My parents were always buying me stuff like that would make everything okay. It worked for them, but it never worked for me. Then we all went on holidays but my nanny came so Mum and Dad could go out or whatever they did. I felt like... I felt like an ornament, or an accessory. They had me because all their friends had one, and that's what families do.' My eyes flicker to the box of tissues, but they're just out of my reach. I'd have to make an obvious show of getting one, so instead I focus on the rug, tracing the patterns in my head.

'So you felt very alone growing up.' Well duh, that's what I just said. 'But when you were with your parents, did you get on well?'

My head shakes slowly, automatic, before I have a chance to articulate a response.

'Not Mum. I think Mum was disappointed that I wasn't the little princess that she wanted. I'd rather go visit museums with Dad than get my hair done with Mum and I think that upset her a lot. But Dad's really distant now. He still keeps in touch, from time to time, but I think he feels like he's not part of my life anymore. Or something.' Or something, because it's obvious I've thought long and hard about my family. I don't need her to tell me that it's fucked me up. So what can she say? Well done, I've figured it all out. I need her to help, need her to tell me what to do next.

'To what extent do you think this contributed to the eating disorder that you mentioned?'

'It's not like I ever really thought about it. I never woke up and thought, "Hey, I'm gonna be an anorexic today." It just started with a loss of appetite. I never wanted to eat, so I ended up losing weight. It just makes sense.' I'm painfully aware of the nonchalance I'm trying to project with a shrug. 'But...as I got skinner, my mum noticed me more. I went from a size 12 to a size 6 in next to no time. That's pretty much halved in size. Mum liked me better that way. She wanted to spend more time with me. As an older teenager she could talk to me more, took me out for manicures and pedicures. We got our hair done together, went for cocktails in the afternoon and she used to take me to all these parties, like a trophy daughter. She loved that people oohed and aahed about her daughter. That I was doing well in school was like an added bonus – all Mum's friends are airheads.' Looking at her, I wonder how much might fit into Mum's world. With that brown turtle neck and the strings of costume jewellery there is no way Mum would ever have the time for her. She'd probably consider my counselor as one of the more 'unfortunate' people of the world.

'And what did you think about this way of life that your mother introduced you to?'

'Hated it.' Like I needed another second to think of a reply, 'Maybe it was fun at first. I loved the attention – I won't lie. That's what being skinny is all about, right? Mum would love how skinny I was, she'd show me off and I'd feel like I'd actually achieved something for a change. It was the only way that we connected. Size 8, and Mum would lose interest. I started eating, a little more. We were going to dinner parties and stuff. But once I'd upped a size she made me feel like shit.' My glance flickers across the room to a filing cabinet; is swearing allowed? How formal is this?
'Really shit. And she made me realise that I was some kind of fat loser. So the weight came off, went on, came off and then I went to uni.'

She's asking me more questions and somehow I'm answering but the words could be coming from anywhere. Fuck the pretenses, I'm done with wiping my tears on my sleeve and there's only so much sniffling that can be tolerated. Tissues twist in my hand, dampening and falling to shreds on my knee. Something's stuck inside my lungs, despite its attempts to wriggle its way out. My heart is squashed against my rib cage, beating so hard that my body is shaking, my organs rattling. Tears down my cheeks, snot close to my lips, my whole body feels like it's melting. Mum in the car, shaking her head, my 15 year old self clutching at my waist, grabbing fists full of the fat that so offends her. Then I'm two stone lighter, sipping from a glass in a busy bar, tossing my hair and laughing at inane jokes. But everyone is looking at me, everyone needs to see my reactions, hear my opinions. Disappearing, but everyone cares.

'I don't want to go back to that.' My voice feels distant, drifting to a surface while my head remains beneath the water. Wavering and muted. 'I don't want to go back to that.' Clearer, in tones that I know are coming from my own tongue, from my teeth. Touching my mouth to make sure it's real.

She's giving sympathetic nods from across the rug, and I hate how smug she looks with her legs crossed and her sandals. Sandals? It's raining outside. But she's cushioned and cosy, so fuck what's really going on. On my feet now and she's smiling, always nodding, saying something that is probably supposed to sound comforting. But it's condescending because I'm the fucked-up twenty-something and she can go home to her perfect counselling-free life. What a bitch.

'Okay, sure. Thank you very much. Goodbye.' Still, I manage to play the polite guest, conscious of how crisp and gentle my voice can sound. Closing her office door behind her, I leave Carol to her scribblings. I'm at the reception now and a plump, mother-stereotype kindly shows me where the toilet is. In the mirror is a startled face and though the eyeliner hasn't smudged there are puffy red pockets around the eyelashes. Concentrating on concealer, I'm stealing myself the time to breathe, to regulate my heart beat before I go and meet Matt. Putting my make-up away I notice a message from him. He's outside already – somehow I've spent the full forty five minutes in Carol's room.

Matt's just across the street, hands dug into the pockets of his jeans. He's leaning against some railings but once he catches sight of me he straightens up. The hands come out of his pockets and I know that he's ready to hold me, confident that we're on our way to everything being okay. I want to tell him that the counselling was great, that it's really working out and that I feel on top of the world.

'Hey lady, how did it go?' His beaming smile, confidently finding my eyes.

'Yeah, it was...interesting. Useful.' But I can't shirk the feeling that I'm just another sad story, something to remind her to be grateful.

'Well, that's good. When do you go back?' Matt's taken my hand, holding me to a standstill while the traffic goes past. I'm anxious to run and hide.

'In a fortnight.'

'Sounds good. Will we go for something to eat?' Like my counselling is something to celebrate.

I don't want to do it, but...

'Sure.'

How can I break the illusion for him? How can I tell him that maybe his idea didn't work out?

'I know of an excellent Italian restaurant on the bridges.'

'Really?' Feigning interest. It's not that I don't care, it's just that I'm finding it hard to care.

'Yuh. La Bella Pizza Hutta.' Matt laughs at his own joke, leading the way in his happy thoughts. I can't cut him down when he's high – the ground is crumbling as it is.

TWENTY-TWO

Sarah

The room is a collection of pizza boxes and takeaway cartons, the air hot with sweat and grease. Plates and glasses stacked in towers in the corners: the extent of our tidying. On waking I feel nauseated, my nostrils filled with the stench of food long since eaten. Somehow the pizza crusts aren't mouldy, so they're no danger to us yet. Matt's lying curled beside me, clinging close on the single bed. Our skin sticks together and I have to peel myself from him to sit. As I swing my legs over the edge my toes knock over an open bottle of Coke and I stoop to mop the mess with one of my discarded t-shirts. Like living in a pig sty. In fact, I'm sure the relativity of the squalor makes us equal. Actually, perhaps pigs are cleaner.

We're in hibernation; we've surrendered the outside world. Matt's words, not mine. He's right, though. I've never been happier. Here I'm queen of everything - Matt makes me feel gorgeous, I'm always beautiful, the most beautiful. There's no girls to compare to, no crowds to worry me. I don't pick at my face or conceal my freckles, I don't spend hours worrying about how my breasts look in my top, I don't trace the lines of my lips and nose and wonder how I could change them. I'm better than all that.

After all, it's not us - it's them. Them being... family, friends, managers, customers, counsellors and psychologists, passersbys and shop assistants. We've cut out the people that don't matter. A brief, 'Hello' to the Asda delivery guy is perfectly manageable. Taking the pizza from the delivery guy doesn't warrant conversation, and Naomi's so busy with her masters that our lack of chat is barely noticeable. I'm smiling, conscious of how pleased I am that this all works out.

Shit. Matt's phone fully wakes me and I'm scrambling on the floor trying to figure out where the noise is coming from. Beneath my dressing gown by the bookcase. Chris. His manager's calling. Frowning, I tiptoe over the detritus to get to the bed.

'Matt, Matt.' Useless, I know. The boy could sleep through a blitz, 'Matt. Matt. It's Chris calling.' I thrust the phone by his ear, hoping the irritating ringtone will be enough to rouse him. It does, but just as Matt's eyes open the ringing stops.

'Whawasi?' Matt manages to turn himself onto his back, hand brushing my cheek as he reaches for the phone. Eyes barely open, he squints at the screen.

'It was Chris.' There's a gravity in my voice to match the severity of the situation, and sure enough Matt catches it as he sits up.

'Fuck.'

'You can't hide from him forever, you know.'

He throws me a look, and I know he thinks I'm playing the hypocrite.

'I don't see you going to work any time soon.'

'I'm on...leave. I had holiday to take. I'm *supposed* to be off.' Though I'm sure I'd be in bed right now regardless.

'Fuck's sake.' Matt's fingers press at the buttons and he holds the phone to his ear. He says nothing, but I can hear that Chris is angry at the other end. Matt remains silent, giving his replies in the form of twisted faces and raised eyebrows.

I think it's supposed to be funny, like it's supposed to be a joke that he's being irresponsible. The word 'immature' is sounding loudly in my mind, but maybe that's being a little cruel.

'Fine, Chris. Whatever, Chris. Uh huh, uh huh. Okay. Yup. Fuck you.' The 'fuck you' delivered like a friendly goodbye.

I wait, not wanting to pressure him if he's as volatile as the phone call suggests.

'Well, I'm officially a free man.' The phone is tossed aside, Matt's announcement made like nothing of any consequence. There's no need to ask what happened: I know that Matt will offer it up once the thoughts are gathered in his head. Sometimes it takes a moment or two for him to comprehend what's actually going on.

'He sacked me.' That I could have guessed, but there's something disturbing about the nonchalant shrug of his shoulders.

There's a silence that needs to be broken.

'Oh...'

'Yup.' I suppose the whole thing's self-explanatory. Matt doesn't show up for weeks, doesn't even fake excuses after a while, ignores calls and texts from Dan.

'So, what next?'

'What *next*? Sarah, we've got all the time in the world. We can do whatever we want.' Matt surfaces from beneath the duvet, rubbing the sleep from his eyes. Suddenly his expression is busy and bright, and all at once I'm gathered into his arms, my back warm against his chest. 'We can read all the books we want, see all those crappy films we always wanted to see.' Whispering, he cradles his chin on my shoulder, one hand stroking across my hip, 'Long romantic walks at night, feeding the ducks at the pond. We can travel the country so that I can do photoshoots, and you can visit all those castles and graveyards.'

I take hold of his wrists, wrapping his arms around my stomach. My eyelids feel heavy, like I'm drowsy under the influence of his promises. I imagine snowfall in a city, somewhere fresh and new for us both. I imagine Matt smiling, taking photographs as I wander through museums. I see Matt being caught for taking pictures where he shouldn't, both of us running between display cases only to arrive laughing breathlessly outside. And spring time, and the flowers. Always Matt, and always me. Everything proofed on his camera. 'All the time in the world...' The words feel warm on my tongue as I sound them out. He presses a kiss to my neck and it breaks the spell.

'But what about money? How are we going to afford that?'

Matt's arms fall limp, a sigh brushing against my shoulder blade. I twist to see him, knowing very well he'll be brushing a hand through his hair; forward, then back. He brings his hands forward again, lowering them to press his fingers to his eyelids.

'I don't know.' His words rush, accented louder than necessary.

'It's a great idea. It really is. But...we'll need to get to places, find somewhere to stay, or to live.' Pacing my words carefully, because I've thrown a spanner in the works. It's horrible to watch him crash, the way his eyes shift with eager excitement to become murky with disappointment as soon as I open my mouth.

He shakes his head, hands covering his face. Though not entirely, his lips moving gently; either talking to himself or...cursing me.

'Matt, it's not that I -' Reaching out a hand, careful, careful...

'Benefits.' His face emerges, shoulders cracking as his arms stretch towards the ceiling. 'Pretty sure I'm "unfit for work" as it is. You could just sign on, or like...get your parents to pay or something. You know your mum would.'

Guilt-trip Mum into paying for my travels. Although it's something I've done before, it's not something I'm willing to do again. Mum would invite herself along, suggest Barbados, "treat" me to Disneyland, Orlando.

'Maybe.' But really, he's right. I've got money saved, tucked away for rainy days. And these are the rainiest days I've ever had. Why not fuck it? Why not throw it all to the wind and just go for it?

'We're only gonna live once.'

Exactly what I was thinking.

'So where to first?' Warmth is bubbling up in my chest, and I'm really looking forward to something. Real life is about to begin, I can tell.

TWENTY-THREE

Matt

Raking through Sarah's drawers, sure that he saw the little silver packet somewhere. Finding anything in this mess is pretty much impossible, so he's going at a slower pace, systematically moving from bookcase to desk. Now he's on his knees, reduced to searching through clothes dumped weeks ago and mugs now growing modest germ-farms. Several of Sarah's handbags to go through and he catches a glimpse of foil. Paracetamol. There's four left, but he takes two, just like the doctor orders. He stuffs the other two into the pocket of his jeans for later, so that he can feel the reassurance of them there. Resigned in his mission, Matt retreats to the bed, ready to sleep out the headache and the trauma. His hand reaches up beneath the assortment of pillows, fingers grazing against plastic. Meds! Still lying, he pulls the packet into the musty daylight of the room. He's no princess with a pea. Each of the little dimples is empty. Fuck. He turns it over, double-checking that there's nothing hiding beneath broken foil. Nothing. Tossing the packet on the floor, Matt thinks of the capsules in his pockets. Maybe they'll alleviate some of the tension, if not the lucid nightmares.

He lifts himself from the bed and navigates his way around the mess to the door, pulling it open as far as it will go and slipping into the corridor. It looks completely different in the afternoon - the objects have more colour, more shape. Everything is brighter and the phone on its stand looks more necessary, the little shelf for shoes seems important.

He's met by Naomi in the kitchen, eyes wide and cheeks red as she discovers his half-naked body. Stammering, she attempts a small greeting, busying herself with the sandwich she was making. Matt nods, running a hand over his gristly face, trying to rub out her image. He knows that she lives there, it's just interesting to see her. He doesn't move further than the threshold, and Naomi cuts her cucumber with solid concentration.

'Would you like something to eat?'

He doesn't voice his answer, but she can feel his negative response as his head shakes heavily. Matt pads across the kitchen tiles, fetching a glass from the sink. Through the headache he turns the tap too hard, spraying his stomach with cold water. His teeth are clenched, any number of curses reduced to a guttural grumble. Rubbing the water into his skin, Matt realises that he probably needed a shower anyway. No big deal. No big deal. On repeat.

From the freezer he locates some ice cubes from behind some tubs of Ben and Jerry's. Several fish-shaped cubes pop from the blue rubber and into the glass. Quick now, before the ice melts, Matt retreats to the bedroom, nodding a goodbye to Naomi though she probably doesn't see, she's buttering her bread so intently.

Back in bed, and suddenly everything's safe again. Just Matt and the mattress; everything necessary for living. The glass is placed carefully on the floor while he digs for the paracetamol, plastic scratching his thigh. Failing to pierce the packet with his grubby nail, he presses hard from the other side, like you're supposed to, like the instructions say. But fuck it to the medical precautions; it's all made up stuff anyway, to cover the doctors in case something goes wrong. If his heart stops or if he grows an extra leg, his GP can say, 'well you read the leaflet' and 'I told you so'. Onetwothree, one big gulp. He sucks his bottom lip between his teeth, biting as he scoops the ice cubes from the glass. He clutches the melting fish in both fists, closing his eyes and concentrating on the pain, forcing himself to hold on and hurt. All pain, no gain, and no scars. She'll never know. Satisfying, releasing the tension, letting the water drip down his forearms as he rests his back against the wall, curling up his feet like a happy child clutching onto his new favourite toy. A light up yoyo.

A light up yoyo, smashed by a friend. A light up yoyo and pulling the string as far as it will go. Wrapping it around his wrists, a game he plays alone in his room. Watching as everything changes colour - his wrist, his fingers. Trying and failing to feel his fingers. A light up yoyo, unwound and wrapped about his neck, pulling tighter at the broken plastic, the light that won't even flicker. Tight around his voice box, feeling the string snug between the grooves. Mum shouting up for dinner, dinner! Matt trying harder to make his head numb, making it disappear just like his fingers. Mum running up the stairs, Mum opening the door, Mum staring at alarm at her eight year old son. Matthew! Matthew! Oh my *God!*

Something stirs beside him, heavy cloth brushing across his shoulder. Sarah. Sarah still has her coat on, bringing with her the scent of a winter turning to spring. The smell of mud, and the scent of bouquets and bunches from work. Matt inhales deeply, a watery smile pulling his lips apart. Sarah smells like a garden.

'You smell like a garden.'

From behind him, Sarah's arm reaches round, resting a small hand on his waist.

'Did I wake you?'

'Mmm...maybe.' He doesn't know, but he knows that his hands are damp and cold. Grudgingly, Matt opens his eyes, looking at the wet patch on the pink sheet. 'Shit, must have spilled my water.' Bring attention to it now, and Sarah won't even have time to ponder anything else. Mention it before she has the chance to think about it; Matt knows it works.

'Don't worry about it. They probably need changing anyway.'

Probably is an understatement. The sheets are discoloured - tea, crumbs, sweat, sex. Weeks of sleep and restless dreams. Time is lost for Matt now, but he's learning to exist without it. There's no clock in Sarah's room, and Matt's phone ran out of battery days ago. Probably days ago. Pretty much. Sleep isn't regulated by a morning and a night, just wakefulness and unconsciousness. Time only exists on evenings and weekends, when Sarah can keep an eye on the hours on her mobile phone.

Sarah slips from the bed, removing her scarf and coat and hanging them over a chair, covering a sturdy mountain of dirty clothes - once worn, now ignored, mostly Matt's.
'So...Lisa came into the shop today.'

'Lisa?' What does she want flowers for? The question is of confusion, rather than interest.

'Yeah...She was wondering if we wanted to go for dinner on Saturday. Get out the house.' She still hasn't turned to face him, deciding now to pick up some of the rubbish from her desk.

'Get out the house? We're not invalids.' Matt's on his feet, making the bed proving that he's still useful; he doesn't need to be cared for. 'What did you say?'

'Maybe... I mean, it's not like we've got anything planned.'

'What about our travelling? Did you forget about *those* plans?' Cuddly toys are haphazardly rearranged, tossed into the corner at the end of the bed.

'*Those* plans,' so carefully copying Matt's intonation, 'were *mentioned* two weeks ago. I thought you were "desperate" to go do that stuff. But you're still here, still doing nothing.'

'Great, so Lisa's been turning you against me.'

'What does that even mean?' Sarah stops stuffing dirty clothes into the laundry basket.

'She just waltzes into your work one day, tells you to go for dinner and decides that you need to "get out the house". We get plenty of fresh air - it's not like we're just sitting around getting fusty.'

'That's not what she meant.' She pauses, swinging the desk chair round to sit, facing Matt. 'But she's right. I mean, we've not gone out together for ages. Months or something. When was the last time we did?'

'New Year's Eve.' Matt's breathes the words slowly, curling up on the bed and taking Pedro into his hands.

Sarah bows her head, digging her finger nails to push back the cuticles. She could be remembering any part of the night, but she's clearly not smiling.

While the awkward memory lingers above their heads, their hands keep busy like they might achieve some reasoning by picking dirt from nails, or pulling the bowtie on a soft toy penguin. There are no apologies, false or otherwise. No taking back any of the words passed between them. Just mutual understanding, an instant acknowledgement of feeling.

Matt is stuck. New Year's Eve will always exist. The turn of the decade will always be the same to him. And Sarah will always remember it too: this is the worst part. Memories are itemised inside his brain, stored away in case of future reference. But there's no erasing Sarah's thoughts, no hiding things best left unseen. If there was a way of patching them up, layering him and burying the bad beneath the good...

'So let's plan our trips. Let's sit down and really do this.' Matt meets Sarah at the desk, reaching into a drawer stuffed full of paper and an abandoned diary. 'Come on.'

A space is cleared on the floor, clothes pushed away into landslides and pizza boxes hidden beneath furniture. Matt sits, opens the diary and flicks through the pages, staring at numbers, days, months. Sarah lowers herself beside him, taking a pen from her handbag. Matt's smile has renewed energy, a rediscovered sense of adventure.

'Alright, Captain Clarke, what's the plan of action?'

TWENTY-FOUR

Matt

A knock at the door, heard faintly above the buzzing of the electric razor. Matt pauses and moves the shaver away from his jaw, waiting to be sure he isn't just hearing things. The knocking is more persistent and Matt unlocks and opens the door, presenting his half-shaved face to a fully-bearded Dan.

'So he is still alive, the little fucker.'

Matt presses the switch on the razor, dipping them into silence; the darkness of the hall behind Dan reminds Matt that 2.00a.m. is not the usual time for shaving. 'Just about.'

'So where the fuck have you been? You could have been dead, for all I knew. For all anyone knew. No one at work has heard from you in like a month. I only guessed you were alive cause Chris told me you quit. *Shit.*' The last word seethes from Dan's teeth in a frustrated hiss. Hands firmly in the doorframe, he creates an accusing cross shape.

Matt takes a step back, affronted by the confrontation. His finger circles the power button, absentmindedly pressing it on and off again. 'I've been staying at Sarah's.'

'Oh, sure, so that explains everything. Why didn't I think of that? "My psycho bipolar flatmate has gone missing. Oh!

He must just be living somewhere else."'

Matt blinks before rubbing a finger into his left eyelid, 'Exactly. It's not so unreasonable. What the hell did you think had happened?'

'Like I said, my psy-cho bi-po-lar flatmate. So fuck knows.'

'Sorry, Mum. Didn't know I had to inform you of my every move. I'm not a kid and I'm not,' Matt steps back, clutching onto the bathroom door, muscles clenching in preparation to slam it, 'an invalid.'

Dan's foot is in the door; there's no way his sizeable calf will let Matt slam that door in his face. 'Whatever. You're sick, Matt. On pills, seeing doctors.'

Matt wants to open his mouth, to declare that medication is a thing of the past; but he deems it unwise, turning to reach the bathroom sink.

'Think you'd let a cancer patient fuck around and go missing for months on end and just let it go?'

It's hardly the same. The shaver buzzes again and Matt pulls the thing through beard and foam, careful to keep his hand relaxed.

The door swings and clicks shut, Dan letting it close as he stands by the sink, a cheek and an eye visible behind Matt's reflection. In the mirror both men stare, watching Matt's gradual transformation. Matt turns the razor off and drops it into the sink, blinking at the new contours of his face. Despite all the shit he's been eating, despite all the rest, his face has faltered with his mind. Blue eyes are blue, but seem to be lacking something. The jaw and cheek bones are more pronounced, pasted with milky white skin like a papier-mâché mask. He lifts a shaky hand, wiping the remaining foam from his cheek before it drops to his chest.

'You *fucking* idiot.'

Matt sees the venom in Dan's creased brow and clenched teeth, he feels the quick movement coming from behind him. Not fast enough, Matt watches Dan's fist swing for his face before closing his eyes on impact.

Dan's arm around Matt's throat. Matt's fingers grasping at Dan's wrist. Matt and Dan hit bathroom tiles. Matt elbows Dan near the throat. Dan pins Matt. Dan throws punches. Matt's eyes. Matt's nose. His jaw, his cheek, his arm, his stomach. Fragile Matt, pale and exhausted. Breathing hard on the cold bathroom floor. Curling into a foetal position, clutching at his stomach. Breathing. Breathing. Harder. Softer. Choking, gargling at the back of his throat. Spit. Blood. Red blood, blue tiles, blue eyes, white face.

Dan's sitting on the edge of the bathtub, head between his legs. Someone's going to be sick. Between friends, between vomit and spit and blood. Each struggling to share the air in this small room.

Matt doesn't attempt to move, just cradles himself by the

toilet, focusing on the toilet brush to stop the world from spinning.

'You're a fucking idiot.' Dan shakes his head between his knees before lifting it to look at Matt, to really take note of the damage done. It's a sorry sight - a friend, struggling, wriggling on the floor like a worm cut in half. His words are heavy and toned apologetically.

'Don't you give a shit? Did you never stop to think that there were people actually worried about you?' Curses whisper in mumbles from his lips, 'I know, I get it. I know you're having a tough time of it but *shit* man, you can't do this to us.'

Us. Who is us? Us is Dan, Sue, Chris, Johnny, a family who've never questioned lack of communication in the past few months. Us is the medical centre, the psychologists. Us is all the people who aren't Sarah. Matt hauls himself to sitting, resting a throbbing cheek against the rim of the toilet, a hand reaching for the toilet brush, just for extra tactile assurance.

'And beating the fuck out of your "psycho" flatmate is going to help him, how?'

'Never heard of the phrase, "Knock some sense into you"?'

'I'm not sure it's meant to be taken quite so literally...' Matt gathers spit in his mouth, swirling around his teeth and gums before spitting into the toilet bowl: it lands in the water, tainted pink.

'Matt, you're a state. Look at the nick you're in.' Dan sighs, pressing his palms against the bath edge while deciding between staying and standing. 'You used to have it made. A little job, decent flatmate, good friends, photo gigs on the side. That's pretty good going by anyone's standard. And then...' Dan stands to his feet, prepared lest his words send his friend reeling with energy. 'Then Sarah came along. I mean, she's cute and all but she's just not -'

'I'm not taking this shit from you.' Husky and soft, Matt's voice and legs wobble as he tries to get to his feet. He's suddenly reminded of a scene from Bambi, and shuts up immediately for fear of just looking ridiculous. He leans heavily on the metal handle, the flush gurgling loud enough to be the last word in their conversation.

'You need help.' Dan dares himself to speak above the quiet whirr of water. 'And I'll help you get help. Seriously.' He coughs, abashed by how difficult open honesty can be.

'Thanks.' Matt turns on the taps, cupping his hands full of water and splashing it over his face. He leans into the mirror, examining the damage - swollen lip, bruised cheek, and the likelihood is that his left eye will be purple by the morning. He turns sideways, looking for the source of pain on his upper bicep. Matt tentatively presses at the swollen scars, white and puffy.

Dan drifts into view of the mirror, his own eyes focused on the faint criss-cross patterns.

'Looks like someone got carried away with noughts and crosses.'

He bows his head, hiding his eyes, immediately embarrassed by his own nervous joke. The temptation is to stare: he always knew they were there, he'd just never seen them before, not in the stark white light of the bathroom.

'Fancy sitting up with a beer for a bit?' Matt's voice is half-lost inside the towel scrubbing into his face.

But Dan's restless, already standing with the door open, 'I'd better get to bed.'

'Sue in?'

'Nah, she's out. Some girly cocktail night or something.'

'Right.' The two share sympathetic looks, perhaps the first sign of real camaraderie in months. In the dark hallway they stand in front of their respective bedroom doors.

'How about tomorrow? We could get pizza?'

Dan scratches the edge of his receding hairline, 'I've got work early, then I said I'd take Sue out for dinner. Y'know, pay day and a Friday and all that.'

'Friday. Yeah, of course. Right.' Time does still exist, and it matters for many people. Days have only slipped away from Matt. He shivers; it's cold, and it's frightening to know that he's out of such an essential loop.

'Well, night then.'

'Night.'

'Good to have you back, man.'

'Yeah, you too.'

Matt's bedroom is much how he remembered it to be. He's surprised to think just how much smaller it seemed last winter, how much darker. The desk lamp goes on, illuminating the edges of a forgotten about photo display: the Meadows in black and white - trees at the point of turning brown, squirrels and conkers, swings and roundabouts.

How loud does a call for help need to be? Matt curls up on the duvet, warming his arms beneath the pillows, still smelling of the perfume Sarah wore in the late autumn. So much depends on that drink of beer, the banter and chat broached on a sofa. So useful would be a lazy day, discussing depression, all eyes on the Xbox. Or the comfort of pizza and a full stomach for asking about help. Somewhere in the bedroom is a list of numbers and websites from his GP; people to talk to at times like these. There's probably several, but fuck knows where they are. It would have been a smart move to put some in the Batman tin.

He dials the only number he knows.

'Ung? Hellu?'

'Sarah, it's Matt.'

'Oh!' Her alert voice amuses him, and he imagines her sitting up in bed, grabbing at a cuddly toy while she listens. 'Is everything okay?'

Difficult question. The answer is no. In every which way the answer is no.

'Yeah, yeah, everything's fine. I was just thinking, we should do it tomorrow.'

'Tomorrow?'

'Tomorrow. If you get your bags ready and stuff, I'll come meet you in the morning and we can head down to the bus station ASAP.' He sounds out the acronym as if it were just a word.

'Oh...alright. Do you have a plan?'

'Nope! It'll be an adventure! Are you excited? I'll see you tomorrow morning, okay?'

'Okay.'

'I love you.'

'I love you too.'

'Goodnight.'

'Ni' night.'

Tomorrow morning everything will be different. Sarah and Matt will be in a completely different world - where no one even needs to ask for help. No help needed. Nothing to rely on - no drugs, no counsellors, no therapy. Just Sarah and Matt. The world is their oyster, and they're ready to fetch the pearl.

TWENTY-FIVE

Matt

'What do you mean, she's not here?' Naomi cuts an impressive figure, a wall between the staircase and the warm corridor.

'She told me to meet her.' Matt takes a bold step forward, but he's more likely to be stuck between her breasts than push past her. '*Please.*'

'Okay. You can go look if you have to but really, she isn't here.'

Matt finds it hard to believe Naomi, but given the distance between the front door and Sarah's bedroom there's no reason for Naomi to lie. After all, Sarah always said –

But Sarah's not there. The bed is made; still the same duvet and pillowcases as there had been for the past month or two, but tidied with Pedro in pride of place. Pizza boxes and empty bottles are gathered in various plastic carrier bags that sit beneath the desk, like that is their proper place and where they should go. The room looks much bigger now that all the clothes have been scooped from the floor and shoved in a teetering pile on a chair. Matt leaves the room, and Naomi's still lingering by the front door: she knew he wouldn't find Sarah here, he knew that. But seeing is believing, right?

'Has she gone to work?'

Naomi glances at her wrist, but she's wrapped in a tattered blue dressing gown and her arms are bare. 'At this time in the morning? Matt, it's six a.m.' The number six is heavily stressed, and Matt is reminded that no one in their right mind likes to be awake at that hour.

'Fuck.' Matt pulls his phone from his jean pocket, shaky fingers scrolling down a short list of names. 'C'mon Sarah, where are you?' Words barely whispered while an impatient Naomi rolls her eyes and pads back to her bed.

'Sarah, where - ?' Her answering machine message. Nothing fancy, just your average leave-your-name-and-number chat. The word "message" is cut short at the end. Sarah's always asking people to leave their mess.

'Sarah? Sarah, it's Matt. Listen, where are you? I thought we were meeting here, at your flat, but I guess I might have got it wrong? Anyway, call me back when you get this message. I'll probably be at your flat. Okay, good. Well, see you soon.'

He's aware that his voice wavered in tone and pitch and the end of his voicemail, and he makes a mental note to clear his throat before he starts next time. Hands sweaty, forehead hot, Matt unhooks his camera bag from his shoulder, slings off the empty rucksack and drags his way back into Sarah's room. His room. Their room. It was their room; it was like their home. But Sarah's not there. As he removes his coat and drops it over Pedro's head it becomes uncomfortably quiet. Naomi's not even snoring, for once, and there's no ticking from Sarah's wrist watch. Matt holds his phone with both hands, sinking down on the bed and staring at the screen, waiting for a flash or a bleep.

'For fuck's sake, Sarah...' He gives himself a second or two to go over all the possibilities of her whereabouts in his head, but he's exhausted at the count of three. Matt thinks of nothing. There's no possible reason in the entire world for Sarah's disappearance. Four hours ago, a little over that now, four hours ago and he'd heard her voice; she'd agreed on the phone. This time he hadn't made it up.

'Sarah.' The name hisses from behind clenched teeth and the phone is tossed aside in the realisation that only two minutes have passed. Matt forces himself to his feet, pacing around the room and pulling back the curtains, taking a peek just in case she was waiting there for him. He thinks about all those books and films where men pace around the room, gaze out of windows, or dangle over the fireplace, and he wonders if they're feeling the same torment that he is now. Just waiting...for a decision, an action, a lover.

Was it possible she'd left a note? The surfaces of Sarah's room are still a picture of chaos; phone bills, takeaway menus, empty envelopes and piles of discarded letters; doctor appointments, bank statements, the occasional cursory note from her mother. But if she was going to leave any kind of note, surely she'd put it somewhere she'd be sure he'd see it. Matt stands in the centre of the floor, inching himself round to do a steady 360 of the room. Nothing.

'What the fuck, Sarah? What the *fuck*?' Swearing in the hope it'll calm him down, but the moment the words leave his mouth his heart only beats faster, harder. He has another go at calling and nearly bites his tongue as her phone doesn't even ring, just clicks straight to voicemail. With every effort he holds his breath, just breathing after the tone in case she appears from nowhere. But she can't be nowhere. She *has* to be somewhere. The phone is thrown to the floor, the back falling off to expose the battery.
'Shit.'

There's one last chance - the drawer she keeps her nail polish. He knows she keeps the address book there because after the whole thing with the Forth Road Bridge, she'd asked him to write any more numbers in there. So he was worth keeping tabs on, but now she'd just disappeared. It didn't even occur to Matt that he should feel disappointed; he just felt hot, bitter, and really fucked off that she hadn't kept her word. Searching straight to the letter C: just above his own scribbled details was Sarah's neater print and a small love heart after Gran and Grandad Clarke. Love hearts in Sarah's alphabet are used only in matters of extreme importance. She isn't the kind of girl to put them anywhere. Hearts existed after she wrote his own name, and here was one beside her grandparents' - so they were the ones that she actually liked. On her Dad's side. Figures. He takes the small floral notebook to the bed, pressing the back of the phone into place. Matt begins pushing the buttons of an unknown area code, but it's barely seven in the morning. Can't panic old people at seven in the morning. But then -

'Hello?' Matt imagines the voice will belong to Sarah in fifty years' time.

'Hello. Is that Mrs Clarke?' He can't help but smile, pleased at how eloquent he can sound when he has to. 'I'm a friend of Sarah's. I was just wondering if you'd heard from her at all recently? Oh, no. No need for alarm. Uh huh. You see, I was supposed to meet her this morning but she hasn't shown up yet.'

'How did you find this number, dear?'

Fuck. Didn't think of that. 'Oh... I found it in her address book.'

Even frailer voices can turn cold and stern,.

'And why would you have Sarah's address book? *Who are you?*'

'My name is Matthew, Mrs Clarke. I'm Sarah's boyfriend.' His eyes screw closely together, concerned for his safety in this conversation with a worried grandmother.

Some mumbling on the other end and Matt tries to picture the woman's face, hearing the phone being exchanged from her hand to another.

'Hello! This is Mr Clarke.' A sentence expectant of some kind of important reply.

'Hello Mr Clarke, I'm sorry to interrupt you at this time in the morning.'

'I'm quite awake. What can I do for you?'

'I was just curious if you had heard from Sarah. I can't get through to her phone.'

'And are you quite sure she's not at home fast asleep? Hm?' Matt was willing to bet that at some point in life Granddad Clarke had been a school headmaster. Demon.

He shuffles back on the empty bed, resting his back against the wall.

'Yes. I've checked at her flat.'

'Boy, Sarah's on her way to come and visit with us. I don't understand why she wouldn't have told you. *Unless*, of course, she had any reason not to?'

'Oh no, sir,' at risk of sounding like a school child. 'We were due to do some travelling together this morning.'

'Well, it would seem she's done her travelling on her own. I'll let her know you were in touch, and perhaps you will hear from her soon. Have a good day, now. Goodbye.' No room for arguing, the phone clicks to a decisive buzz.

'Fucking bastard!' Louder than necessary, forgetting his place, throwing his phone against the wall like it was the old man's fault. *Dick.*

'Ticket for Elgin.' The expression behind the counter is lifeless but in every fairness the words are rushed, scrambled in exasperation. 'Elgin. Ticket to Elgin.'

'Sorry?' At least it blinks, this empty face behind the glass.

Matt leans closer, bowing his head so his lips are closer to the little metal speaker with the holes, 'El-gin. You know?'

Another blink. The assistant's name badge is squint, brightly introducing him as Brian. 'To Elgin? Emm...' What he's looking at is anyone's guess, turning to blink at a screen, reaching to grab at a timetable.

For fuck's sake. 'Inverness? Will that work?'

There's a flicker of light in Brian's eyes as he turns into professional school-leaver.

'Inverness. Is that a single or return?'

'Single, single. I just need to get there.'

Matt turns off to Brian's boring Megabus patter, grabbing notes from his jeans' pocket and pressing them on the sweaty silver plate between them. Scrabbling for the change, Matt leaves half the coins behind in his rushed attempts to find the gate for Inverness. London,

Dunfermline, Glasgow, Inverness. His prayer to God is brief but full of cursing as he reaches the queue which is starting to steadily load onto the bus. His rucksack is tossed to land haphazardly beside large suitcases and camping gear. Groups of travellers are getting settled up and down the bus, taking off coats, grabbing pillows and searching through carrier bags of treats. There's little to no room for manoeuvre and Matt's tucking in and around fat, elderly ladies and acned teenagers with baseball caps. There's a couple of girls eyeing some seats at the back, but they're going nowhere - not if Matt has anything to do with it. And in seconds he's worming his way into a window seat, removing his jacket and dumping it firmly in the seat beside him. Resting his head against the cool window, closing his eyes, wanting to fall into a deep sleep...

'Kerry! Kerry! Over here!' One of Matt's eyes open to see two girls in front of him; giggling, shorts too short for March, a shop-full of plastic bracelets littering their arms. This Kerry, she wriggles her way towards them. She's evidently one of the gang, if a couple of dress sizes bigger. Doesn't stop her from wearing outfits like her friends, unfortunately.

'Excuse me?' An unsure pause. Matt's eyes are closed, but he knows the girls are crowded and staring at him, trying to pull him into some kind of conversation.

'Yeah?' He pulls himself to sit upright, arms firmly wrapped around his chest.

'Mind if I sit here? Just, I want to sit with my friends.'

Matt attempts to see around her, and as far as it would seem, she's either going to sit way at the front beside some old guy, or plonked beside himself. He says nothing, just picks up his jacket from the seat with a flourish that would suggest that he's doing her a huge favour which, all things considered, he feels he really is.

'Thanks.' She gives the smile, flutters the eyelashes, but her eyes roll in their sockets as she flumps down next to him, her gratitude revealed with bitter tones.

Matt nods, hoping to high Heaven that his mp3 player is still in his coat pocket. The bus shifts as the engine starts up, Matt's forehead shaking against the rumbling window pane. Already the girls are loud and raucous, recounting ridiculous stories of drunken nights out, passing round a dog eared magazine with an average-looking model on the front. Matt flicks through the library of songs on his mp3 player, looking for a suitably loud band. He stuffs the headphones deep into his ears, turns the volume up as high as necessary, and closing his eyes with a scowl rests his head against the window.

TWENTY-SIX

Sarah

Here, I am nowhere. Completely removed from everything unsafe, everything scary about the world. The tadpoles are swimming below the surface of the murky pond, some kicking with new legs. Spawn collects in bubble clouds, each bubble with a small black eye; it's so tempting to reach out and touch it - but knowing they'd be destroyed so easily stops me. Grass is damp beneath my toes: my shoes and socks are removed so that I can feel the ground at my feet, and it's comforting to know that it's there. A hawk, a buzzard, some kind of predator swoops across the trees above me and his call joins the choir of birdsong - the only noise there is to hear for miles.

Peace. Really and truly, this is peace. Stillness, quiet, my heart beating regularly, my mind as empty as it can possibly be; content just to *be*. This is being, more than existing. Careful that I don't lie in any mushrooms or molehills, I'm relaxed enough to stretch out across the grass, conscious that I'm not interested in the state of my jeans or coat. Is it any wonder that people were sent to the country for the good of their health in years gone by? It works: a change of scenery does wonders for a change of heart.

Silence is broken by a distant shout, someone calling in warning, or for attention. The words are too faint to be heard; strong vowels but I can't make out the consonants. He could be yelling for anything: gun shot, tree felling, hunting dogs. Safer to investigate, I pull my shoes back on, ignoring the laces and tucking my socks into my jacket pockets. Best to keep to the driveway, keeping clear of the woods and the overgrown foxgloves. A girl is always less likely to come to harm if she keeps to the path, after all. I walk along quickly, but not too fast; I don't want to run into something I shouldn't, be it deer or rifle.

But there it is; a figure desperately trying to conquer the anti-climb paint on the gate. The wrought iron fencing is huge, designed to keep animals in and people out. But he's still trying. He falls a significant height, body contracting into a ball as it hits the ground. My heart's beating ten times faster at the sight of him - there is no mistaking the movements, those limbs.

'Matt?' Still too far away for him to hear me, but as he pulls himself to stand, I know that he has seen me.

'Sarah!' The same cry as before, but clearer now.

I stay rooted where I am, caught in headlights and unsure of where to go. Part of me wants to tear away into the trees, get lost among the undergrowth. Some part wishes I would walk away. But deeper still is the urge to go to him, finding and rescuing. God only knows how he got here. All that matters is that he is here. I'm not sure how long it takes, but eventually I get to the gate where Matt stands with his fingers curled round the iron, a prisoner desperate to get...in? Out?

'Sarah,' his expression softens are he pronounces my name, 'Where - Why did you go? I thought...'

He's struggling to put his thoughts together into a coherent sentence; that's when I know that serious turmoil is bubbling beneath the surface. I'm staring at a mole trap at the side of the driveway, too scared and ashamed to even look at him. I was never expecting a confrontation. What the fuck made me think that if I left him he'd be free and easy without me?

'I thought we were supposed to be going away *together*. Didn't realise you'd be making a head start.' His goofy smile brightens his words and while still staring at the mole trap, I know his expression exactly. Only, when I look at him, I'm not prepared for the manic look in his bloodshot eyes, the deep lines and puffy redness. Our eyes can't meet, and Matt bows his head, kicking at the bottom of the gate like a disappointed school child.

'Why did you run off like that?'

'I needed to get out. I just...couldn't be there anymore. I couldn't deal with it.'

'With what? We were running away anyway, that was the whole point. Only a few more hours and I'd have been there too.' He chokes over the end of his sentence, reaching a hand to scratch at the back of unkempt, greasy hair. 'What was it really that you "couldn't deal with"?'

It's static shock when our eyes do meet; widening eyes and a tugging heart. Forehead pressed against the cool black iron, we're just pupils expanding and contracting. Nauseated. I feel suddenly really sick. My hands find Matt's as my eyes close, trying to keep me steady. I thought it was Matt I couldn't deal with: the scars, those baby blues. But maybe I'd got it all wrong.

'I don't know, Matt. I don't know.' If I speak those words at all, they come out in a squeak of whimper.

Matt's fingers curl around mine, bone almost crushing bone in determination to keep us here. 'Hey, it's okay. It's okay. Don't worry about it.'

But I didn't apologise, not really. Maybe it was in my voice, but I wonder how sorry I really am. If I could stand here forever, eyes closed to darkness, Matt just holding my hands, I'm sure that I would. I find myself letting go, prising my fingers from his sharp digits. Opening my eyes, I'm met with a similar picture as before, only this time Matt has the smallest of smiles, and a squirrel darts about on the grass beside him. Spot the difference.

'Would you like to come in?' If nothing else, it's common courtesy, and the boy looks suddenly too skinny, too pale, too tired: the same diagnosis my grandparents gave to me.

I feel no different, but among the green and rich and growing, I'm small, and quite embarrassed.

'Yes, please.' There's something wrong with this picture, but I just can't place my finger on it. Instead, I press the code numbers into the keypad and the gates clunk and creak as they begin to open.

'I found it in your address book.' Matt states the obvious; I'd guessed so much anyway. I lead the way along the drive in silence, and it's only a matter of seconds before Matt needs to speak again.

'I'd make a pretty good spy, don't you think? I mean, investigating through files and stuff.'

Mostly, it sounds like he's been snooping. Just as well I don't keep a diary, or there's no knowing what kind of things he might have found. He was looking for the address book, some clues, that's all; choosing not to believe that he was trying to find something incriminating, or bitter.

'Yeah, I guess.'

'Sarah...' His voice drifts towards me, and I turn to see him standing by the empty barn, limbs dropping like he's hanging.

He looks so sad, so grey against the white stone of the barn. My heart is crumbling at the sight of him, my feet shuffling closer, crunching across the gravel. I don't know what to say to him, but I'm sure my heart has turned black with the guilt.

'I'm sorry, Matt. I panicked. It was just so... *confusing*. I suppose I was just scared.' Breathing deeply, my toes touching his, my nose resting against his collarbone.

'I was too. But, y'know, that was the whole point. We were there for each other. I mean, we *are here* for each other.' Matt couldn't possibly be holding me closer, his fingers clawing at my coat to reach my back, and instantly I know that I shouldn't have left, and he's probably fighting a cliché about never letting me go.

'Stay with me, for a little while.' The request sounds pathetic, but it needs to be said.

'I'll stay, so long as you don't go disappearing again.' His fingertips digging between my ribs.

Nodding my agreement, slowly slipping apart, 'Come on, you should come and meet my grandparents.'

Matt takes my hand as we begin the climb to the top of the hill and he slows to watch the sheep grazing in the field, lambs suckling and bleating, attempting to run.

'I kind of already have. I spoke to them on the phone at like, stupid a.m.'

'Uh oh. Bet Granddad took to that nicely.'

'Eh...not so much.'

'He hates being woken up early. He says he was robbed of sleep in his childhood and early life, he was some kind of army general, so he says that now he's retired he gets to sleep as much as he wants.'

Matt laughs, shaking his head slowly as he starts to take in his surroundings, 'Guess that makes sense. Is that the house?'

The little flat isn't necessary ugly, but it's not particularly nice either. Attached are the kennels housing spaniels and labradors.

'That?' It's rude, but I can't help but laugh, 'That's where the gamekeeper lives.'

'You have a gamekeeper?' I'm tugging him up the hill, but he keeps twisting to look at the scenery we've just left behind.

'Well, my grandparents do. You don't honestly think they look after all of this on their own, do you?' The exact amount of land my grandparents own is unknown to me, but between forests and creatures, fields and vermin, it's difficult to imagine how even Jack the gamekeeper manages it all.

At the top of the hill, hidden behind the stretches of trees that I wish I knew the name of (possibly pine, or oak, or chestnut) is -

'Whoa. Fuck me. That's not your grandparents' house?'

My nod is slow, and I say nothing because it's horrible admitting that I know anyone that has the kind of money for a house like that. My parents' house is impressive enough as it is, all my friends half-excited, half-frightened to spend the night there.

'I mean, I knew your family was rich but this is just -' Matt doesn't seem frightened; he's all excitement, taking in the pillars, over-intricate carvings, white bricks, green lawn, windows that sparkle despite the lack of sun. When we reach the garden path, Matt steps aside to let me go first, following after me across the flagstone steps.

'You'd best wipe your feet before you go in.' Wiping my feet, pushing the door open, Matt still scratching his trainers against the welcome mat. In the vestibule my shoes are carefully removed, and I place them on the little wooden shoe rack, next to his and hers pairs of walking boots and wellies. Matt dutifully copies, suddenly silent in the small enclosed space, like he's holding his breath for what's beyond the door. Jackets and shoes removed, I step in front and push the door open.

The entrance hall is huge, boasting that big, big staircase and a series of doors that lead to other wings, other rooms. On hearing Matt's gasp, I take hold of his hand, squeezing his fingers as I head towards the sitting room. As we get closer I'm certain that my grandparents are there, the notes of archaic choral music drifting through the heavy door.

'Hello, Granddad.' Until I look at him, I forget how old he's getting. He never aged, not until I left for university.

Now every time I see him it's like he's aged another ten years all at once. He's sitting on his huge armchair, his feet propped up on a cushioned rest, newspaper sprawled across his thin legs. His arms are folded tightly about his chest as he leans back into his pillows, chin nodding slightly in time with the music.

'Sarah, ah - I see you've brought a friend.' Granddad reaches out a hand to search for his glasses on the arm of the chair and shakes his head to realise that they're hung about his neck.

'And who might this be, hmm?' Grey eyes narrow behind the lenses.

'Granddad, this is my boyfriend. Matt.' I let go of his hand, and I desperately hope that he'll make a good impression. Please don't mess this up.

Matt stands tall, taking a decisive step towards the chair, which causes my granddad to rise from his seat. Their eyes meet, and Matt takes Granddad's small hand in his own, giving a firm but friendly shake. I'm smiling, and giggle a little; it's amusing to watch Matt being so formal, and to see Granddad's reaction to the first guy I've ever presented as suitor.

'Mhmm...pleased to meet you, Matt.'

'And you, Mr Clarke.'

Granddad let loose from Matt's grip, sinks slowly back into his chair.

'Yes, well, Sarah. You've chosen quite the polite young man.' He pushes the glasses further up his nose, a gesture that I connect with crosswords; his concentration face.

The formality is too much for me, reducing me to huge smiles and an overwhelming need to laugh.

'Take a seat, take a seat. Lorna is just putting the kettle on.' Granddad clears his throat, something crackling like it's struggling to get out. 'Lorna! Sarah has a guest with her. We'll be needing more tea. And those biscuits!'

It's horrible to see how much effort it takes: his voice used to be so strong. No one can make out Grandma's response, but the excited quaver of the notes suggest that she heard.

Grandma announces herself with a rattle, Cath Kidston tea set shaking on a tray. She disappears and returns with a matching cake stand, a variety of biscuits set out in patterns.

'Well.' She dusts her hands off and sits herself in the armchair beside Granddad's, and I know it's my cue to get up from the sofa, settling by the coffee table to make the tea just so.

'You must be the young man that called this morning, yes?' Grandma talks sometimes like she's an exaggeratedly genteel housewife, but there's that knowing look in her eye that proves that she's wise beyond all our years combined.

'Uh...yes, that was me. I'm sorry for calling at such a ridiculous time.' Matt's foot is tapping nervously against the antique Persian rug, a toe worrying its way through a hole in his sock.

'So whatever had happened? You seemed awfully confused.' Grandma takes the remote for the CD player from Granddad's chair, turning down the ominous chanting.

'It was just a lack of communication, I suppose.' The toe is tapping faster, and Matt lifts a hand to rake his hair from his face, covering the fact that he's swiping sweat.

In the silence that follows, I concentrate on putting the sugar cubes into Granddad's tea. Lack of communication? That's just stupid, and it doesn't even make any sense. So I just forgot to tell Matt I was getting on a train, and just went off without him anyway? I pass Granddad his cup on a saucer, complete with two of his favourite biscuits. He's looking at Grandma, and they nod simultaneously. Whatever they've telepathically decided between them, they've at least decided to let the problem lie.

'Well, we're all here now, hmm?' At least Granddad is kept happy in the meantime with his custard creams.

'That's right,' Grandma takes her tea and cradles it carefully on her lap. 'And you are free to stay as long as you like. We don't get many visitors up here anymore.' She takes a careful glance at me, 'Not now that your idiot for a father is shacked up in Hawaii. Never so much as an invitation, you realise?'

'He's not invited me there either, Grandma. He's just busy with other things.'

'Well, dear, when you get to our age there is no time to be waiting around.' She lifts the cup tentatively to her lips while my granddad makes a scoffing noise. Neither of us want to remind her that she's not even seventy yet, that Granddad has a good seven or eight years on her. 'Anyway, let's not be rude. Young man -'

'Matt.' Granddad likes to interject with a knowledgeable air.

'*Matt*, how was your journey here? Tell us, what do you *do?*'

All eyes on Matt now, and he's stirring half a digestive round and round his cup, starting at hearing his name, the biscuit dissolving into gunk and dropping into the tea.

'Oh. The journey was...okay. I don't like buses much. It was very busy, very noisy.' My grandparents nod their understanding of his statement - if anyone despises public transport it's these two. 'But I made it. Got a taxi from Elgin, and the man was very friendly.'

Struggling, he's adding details that I know he wouldn't think of otherwise, but he's doing his best to communicate with his elders. As I brush a hand against his thigh, he's nudged into remembering the second question.

'I'm...a...photographer.'

Correct answer. Grandma is fascinated with pictures, and Granddad's bemused with cameras and technology. Matt's shoulders relax, he leans into the cushions, neglects his tea because he's busy talking. Eventually he has to put his cup and saucer back on the table because he's so close to spilling it. Matt gesticulates, pauses to explain things slowly and carefully, guiding my grandparents through uncharted technology. I make another pot of tea, and he's standing behind them now, camera in his hands. He shows off photographs, points at buttons and passes the camera for Grandma to try.

Here is something I'd never imagine: my grandparents and Matt, excited and animated. The three least likely people, all enjoying life, enthralled by the landscapes Matt has caught on film. A renewed energy for life and living. Matt smiles at me, and I dab the tears at my eyelashes.

TWENTY-SEVEN

Matt

'If I were you, I would stay here forever.'

Matt leans against the wooden fencing, clambering up so his feet are firmly on the bottom rung. He watches the sheep; fascinated at the way the families move in groups, ewes casually keeping an eye on newborn lambs. Besides the sheep, everything is green. Barn house, tractors, fields, hills, trees.

'Really?' Sarah's toes kick at a stone, remaining at a disinterested distance from Matt and his view.

'Yeah. I want to go to the top of those mountains.' His head nods beyond the field to the distant hills, coloured in various shapes and sizes of woodland. On hearing a faint sound above him, Matt tips back his head to watch a buzzard swooping in circles. 'I'd kind of like his view, but it's so nice to be just surrounded by nothing but trees and hills, y'know?' Matt is sincere in his clearly felt observations and he turns to see if Sarah shares his enthusiasm.

But her eyes are focused on her boots. She only looks at him when she hears him pause, 'But what about the rest of the world?'

'I don't feel like I need it anymore.'

Joining Sarah, he takes up her hands and presses them between his own, stealing the warmth from her skin. 'Pretty sure there's nowhere else in the world that looks so...I don't know!'

Her hands are let go, and he meanders along the driveway, the old abandoned barn his destination.

'Haven't you ever been this far north before?'

'Nup. The furthest north I've been is probably Fife, and that doesn't really count for much.' Matt's navigating the fences, discovering a mouldy stile; fungus grows happily on the rotten wood.

'Wouldn't you get bored...if you lived here forever?' Sarah slips on the stile, but Matt's ready with steady hands. He holds her, a hand in hers and another at her waist.

'If this was one of those period drama TV-from-a-book things, this would be a really erotic moment.' Matt lifts Sarah, with ease, completely off her feet, only letting her touch the ground when he has her as close as possible. He presses a kiss to her lips; deep and affectionate. He's still holding her when he leaves her lips, his eyes and teeth shining in a smile.

'This is the perfect place to be. I could take loads of photos round here and sell them on calendars and coasters. You could go into town and start up your florist's. Is there really a cuter place to set up shop?'

Excitement is contagious, and as Matt leads her round molehills and fox shit to the old white barn, it does almost seem possible. Something about the empty shell causes Matt to lower his voice, thoughts coming across in whispers.

'We could convert this place and live here. Look,' he points upwards at a remaining beam, a white owl huddled asleep in the corner, 'complete with owls and everything.' Matt waits, watching for some hint of enthusiasm on Sarah's face. It takes a moment, then it's there, and softly she pads across bird droppings and debris to stand in the centre of the building.

'Would I get to decorate it my way?'

'Absolutely! And here could be the living room, with a real wood fire. We'd never run out of fuel.' Matt tiptoes to a square shape in the wall, presumably once a window, 'Look at the size of our garden!'

Sarah shuffles Matt out of the way to take a look at the view. 'Wow. I could grow all my flowers right here.'

Matt just nods, pacing around the floor space like a real prospective buyer, 'Of course, I'll cook for you. Venison I get from the woods, pheasant every other day...'

Their combined laughter fills the ruin, voices reaching up beyond the rafters, ruffling the feathers of the sleeping nocturnal creature. Aware of the disturbance they're making, they smother their giggles with kisses.

'I'd be an *amazing* stay-at-home dad.' Matt's voice murmurs close to Sarah's ear and though he's sure he can feel her smiling against his neck, she says nothing. 'So what do you think?'

Sarah takes a step back, cursing as she stumbles over a stone, or something.

'You okay?'

She's crouching on the ground now, rubbing anxiously at her ankle, 'Yeah. Though, I think I've sprained it.'

Matt squats beside her, cradling her foot carefully in his hands, but the movement causes Sarah to wince, biting her lip in stoic attempts at bravery. 'Come on, let's get you back up to the house.'

Sarah makes a series of moans as Matt gathers her up, an arm about her waist, the other bracing her arm across his shoulder. Outside the barn, the clouds are tinted with pinks and reds, the colours spilling into a darkening sky. 'Red sky at night, shepherd's delight.' Smiling through her pain.

'Is that really real?' They're pacing slowly, more careful than on their walk down. Every few paces, they're forced to rest; Matt acting as Sarah's harbour.

'Jack swears by it.'

'Huh. I'd never stopped to think about it before.' Matt's hand roves over Sarah's back, comforting and warm.

'When was the last time we really looked at the sky?'

A horrible question; simple really, but the weight of answer seems to shut down Matt's heart. It tugs, and the blood is gone - no more breathing. Vaguely, there is the Hogmanay snow: fat fluffly flakes in a flurry. Months later, and he's confronted with red and black, the colours bleeding and merging. January, February, March and nearly April. So many days without a sky. So much time without days.

Here, there is sky, there is a ground beneath his feet, there is growth. A world that moves without him: he has never been here, and yet everything thrives. Everything is where Matt isn't.

Remotely aware that Sarah is waiting for an answer, but he's forgotten the question. Lost in his recalibration of space and time.

Somehow they make it to the top of the hill, Sarah's grandparents bundling out the door to head for the Mercedes.

'They must be going somewhere.' Sarah's remark is obvious, but Matt lets it slide, walking her across to the car. 'Grandma, where are you going?'

She turns, all jacket and shawl.

'We've got a charity dinner tonight -' Her eyes register Sarah's limp ankle, 'My God, what happened?'

'It's just sprained. Don't worry about it.'

'Let me worry about it a little. Make sure you get it in some cold water as soon as you can, to reduce the swelling. Linda has made your dinner and put it in the fridge. She can't be there to cook for you tonight but I'm sure you'll manage.'

'We'll be fine.'

A gruff voice calls from the driver's seat.

'Lorna! Time.'

But the grandmother just smiles and rolls her eyes before turning to Matt with a gracious smile, 'Thank you so much for looking after her. What ever would we do without you?'

Matt smiles, parts his lips lightly in readiness to speak but   -

'Anyway, I'd best be off before I get into trouble. You two enjoy your evening. We won't be back too late, of course.'

Dinner is neglected, better things on Matt's mind. He takes Sarah's hand, doing his best to remember the way back to the bedroom he's staying in. As with age-old propriety, Granddad and Grandma have Matt and Sarah sleeping in separate guest rooms. Sarah's room is the furthest away, a shrine to the small girl she once was - pink everywhere, a real princess' room, a bed surrounded in pink and white muslin, a collection of cuddly toys to rival her room in Edinburgh.

Closer is Matt's room - neither interesting nor unique. Floral wallpaper, baskets of potpourri that have lost their smell. An old print of puppies sat in a straw hat hangs above the bed, the colours fading. Matt and Sarah burst into the bedroom, flashes of colour, youth and life. Sarah's quick to get comfortable on the bed, removing her coat and scooting back, stretching her legs out, feet pointing towards the white trellis ceiling.

'Uhm, what can I get you? Ice, right?' Matt's remembering that he is left with Sarah and a promise he'd make her better. The trek back to the kitchen is by no means quick, but taking two or three steps at a time halves the journey.

The ice cubes are cleverly hidden in a freezer that is disguised by a rustic-looking cupboard front. Fortunately, a tea towel is hanging by a cast iron stove. Does anyone even cook with those anymore?

'Are you okay?' Matt's voice rises a semi-tone as he rewraps the ice inside the cloth.

Sarah nods, shuffling to give Matt space. He squishes into the duck feather duvet, lifting the cold press to Sarah's ankle with a shaky apprehension.

'Better?' Worried that his doctoring skill won't save her, that he can't be a knight in shining armour.

Sarah lies back against the bed, resting her cheek against fluffed up pillows. Most are for decoration only - there's no such thing as a good night's sleep on satin pillows with sequins.

'Mhm,' but Matt can hear a wince behind her voice.

He flops back beside her, propping his head in his hands, eyes down cast on Sarah's face. 'You're so beautiful, you know that?'

The sentiment causes her to blush, though not in the same shade that it did months ago. Still, with her eyes warm, and mousy brown curls twisted over her forehead, when her tongue slips out to lick her lips he catches it with his own smile.

'Better *now?*'

Sarah tips back her head, blinking at Matt with flutters of her lashes. 'Hmm..' Her lips become a lopsided, unsure smile.

Matt wrestles his way on top of her, careful that he doesn't kick her ankle. His attack manifests itself in tickles and kisses, Sarah's body wriggling with Stockholm Syndrome.

TWENTY-EIGHT

Sarah

Screams wake me from my sleep: in a few fuzzy moments I try to decide if the sounds came from my dream or from somewhere closer. The screams aren't mine; the groan of someone being hurt, loud, exasperated cursing.

What's happening?

Stumbling from the bed, my ankle takes my weight and as the pain shoots up my leg I am brought fully round to consciousness. Blink my eyes, and the sleep fog is lifted. Shit. Someone's hurt.

Damn this fucking foot, hobbling down the corridor in the direction of the voice. I know before I get there that it's Matt. There's no use in pretending that it might be anyone else, that something vague has happened to a vague person I've never met.

Red. Red, dripping crimson, bleeding burgundy. Colours oozing between white bathroom tiles. Blood resting between the cracks.

Matt, crook of his neck resting on the bathtub, legs stretched out, redundant. His arm is long, somehow longer than it ever has been. An expanse of skin, blood, flesh that

I've never seen before. Matt's arm is a biology lesson; strange and exposed, parts I can't identify.

Dragging a towel from its warmer, sinking to my knees, blood seeping into jeans I fell asleep in. Wrapping the towel tightly around the forearm, hiding the wound, staunching the blood.

'Sarah.' Matt's face turns, flopping towards me, eyes searching like he's struggling to find my face. 'I guess I cut too deep.'

His lips are dry, his voice is low, crackling somewhere inside his oesophagus. Matt's opposite hand lies palm upwards on his stomach, a hint of silver flashing beneath the garish bathroom lights. My granddad is the only person in the world that buys razors like that - the image on books covers, film posters, the iconic blade. I've never even seen them for sale.

Trust Matt to find them, trust Matt to take one and slice it along his arm. Down the road, not across the street.

'You idiot. You fucking idiot.' In my rage, spit speckles my lips but despite my outburst Matt's eyelids just lower, slowly, heavy, shutting down over his unfocused eyes. 'You fucking selfish prick.' Storming back to the bedroom, swearing loudly at every sore step of my sprained ankle. I bite my lip to prevent an onslaught of ranting, taking a deep breath as I touch 9.9.9 on my phone.

'Hello. Yes. My boyfriend's tried to kill himself what do I do there's blood everywhere and - Okay, okay. Ard-Aulinn. Uh...Urquhart Road, Urquhart Road. Okay. Okay. Be quick.'

I don't want to go back to Matt. Don't want to find him again, sprawled and bleeding like road kill. Something falls, metal crashing across the tiles. What the fuck? Matt's trying to get up, pulling himself up with his good arm at the lip of the basin. All he's managed to do is knock over Grandma's toothbrush holder.

'You need to lie down.' I'm surprised at the venom in my voice, at how cold my command sounds. The doting girlfriend would be crying, mopping her boyfriend's wounds with her hair. In the bathroom doorway, one hand on my hip and the other clutching my phone, I'm the impatient parent with her idiot child throwing a tantrum on the floor.

'Help me.' His plea is small, so simple and yet so dangerously full. Yet, I don't help him, I just watch as he lifts the towel and tries to cover up the cuts. There are more than just one - small abrasions surround the large one in a cluster. My lunch stirs in my stomach, acid rising to my throat. This isn't a scene on the television. I can't turn it off or turn away. But I don't want to. Sickened though I am, I'm drawn to the blood, to the folds of skin peeling from his arm. Above the scents of Grandma's air freshener is that heavy scent of blood. It cracks and pools on the white tiles, snaking from Matt's arm. How am I going to clean up this mess?

'Help me.' There's panic in his tenor tones as his lips move soundlessly, the veins on his neck protruding.

'Come on. Let's get you properly cleaned up.' Matt is heavier somehow. I'm used to his weight on my body, used to his shape beside mine, but pulling him to standing isn't easy, and his arm flops uselessly against his thigh. Where do I take him? I need to put him somewhere, but it's easier to let him rest here, keep the chaos contained, and I sit him carefully down on the toilet seat.

Take the red-wet towel, rinse it under warm water, wring the towel and murky brown water releases down the plug hole. 'I'm just going to clean this up a bit, so it's not a mess when the paramedics get here.'

'What?' Matt lifts his working arm, pressing his fingers deep into closed eyelids.

'I called an ambulance. What did you think?' I'm reminded of that scene in *Beauty and the Beast* where Belle is crouched as she cleans Beast's cuts and thanks him for saving her life. It doesn't quite fit.

'You can't, Sarah...' Matt's voice moves in a whisper, his head tilted backwards, the nape of his neck resting against a home-knitted toilet roll dolly. 'You don't know what they'll do to me...'

'It's out of my hands now, Matt. It's not up to me.'

'My whole life is up to you now. My whole life...'

Does he think that I don't know that? He groans as the towel presses harder against the cut. I kick at the toothbrush holder, sending it crashing into the bath. The same satisfaction as slamming a door. 'What do you want me to do? Do you really want me just to go back to bed and pretend I never noticed?'

I think I almost expect him to answer me, to give an honest reply. But of course, he's just staring, eyes wide and blurred, a tear slipping from a duct.

'What would have happened if I hadn't woken up? You'd just be lying here...bleeding to death.' My heart is swelling in my chest, an uncomfortable size that might burst.

'Matt, *why*? Why would you even...?' Burying my face in his lap, arms clutching at his waist: there's nothing to hold but his belt, my fingers hooking into the denim loops of his jeans.

'I just had to.' His hand on my head, fingers clutching at hair. 'It's not your fault. And it's not...'

But it is his fault. It is his fault.

'...it's not my fault.'

My bottom lip puffs when I bite it too hard, chewing it between my teeth. To fight back a reply, indignant answers that he should have seen a doctor, he should have taken his medication, he should have, *he* should have.

'You should have...'

He sighs, and in that sigh are all the words that he doesn't have the energy to say. And I'm glad he doesn't speak because I don't want to hear it. Matt leans over me, pressing his lips to the crown of my head. Warm. And I thought that he was dead. Nearly dead.

I still don't understand.

Sirens wailing. Sirens fading. Gravel crunch. Matt's hand flops as I move from beneath him, run to the door. 'Hello! He's through here!' Never greeted paramedics before. Let alone at the front door. Stair climb, corridor run, bathroom. Bathroom. Matt's teetering on the toilet bowl, slipping out of conscious.

'Help him!'

But my cry isn't necessary - they're busy already. Bags out, equipment. Speaking words to him. Gentle. Being so gentle.

Matt's moving. Floating? On his back, carried by two men in green.

'Hospital': he's saying something but that's the only word I understand.

A hand on my shoulder.

Matt.

Going....

'Wait! Wait!'

Sharp air. I'm outside. How did I get here? The doors closing on the ambulance.

'Where is he going?'

Hospital. I know that. Where else?

'I need to. I need to go with him.'

Pain in my foot. Fuzzy. Screams, my own.

TWENTY-NINE

Sarah

The evening turns dusky; spring and it's late – just cars heading home. There are some kids playing on the climbing frame, limbs like monkeys, navigating the bars in ways not intended for smaller children. There's two teenaged girls swinging together on the same swing, laughing. I wish I had that teenage lack of concern again, where everything is funny, and every event a possibility of something more. I have the roundabout to myself. The metal edge is cool, but clammy with all the hands of a Saturday afternoon. Slowly I walk round and around until I'm speeding up, toes barely touching the ground, faster and faster until I jump.

Throw myself, and shuffle back, trying to sit safely as it tilts and spins. Edinburgh whirs past quick enough that I have to close my eyes. In books characters say that their head spins, and I wonder if this is what they mean; a wobbling dizziness. I'm suddenly conscious of my body here in the centre of a city moving around me.

Me. Here. Now. I need solidity and I need peace. I want to open my eyes and walk into a world with a place for me – florist's assistant, or a school teacher, a tourist, maybe a wife, or a mother. A role, and a life.

Me, here, a job I might not even still have, absent parents, and a boyfriend who cares enough to -

Stop the world, I want to get off. Words I've heard my father say. Stop. I want to get off.

The roundabout is slowing but still I misjudge the leap down. My knees land heavily into the ground, catching my fall with palms pressed into the dirt. I brush my hands against one another, dusting earth and stones.

As I walk towards the gate, I realise that my stumble hasn't gone unnoticed, and the stares make me hurry away. Reaching for my phone, needing someone, needing friendly understanding.

'Well hello, stranger.' Lisa's voice sounds naturally happy, actually pleased. 'Long time no see! Where the hell have you been all my life?'

Pause as I take a deep breath - what am I supposed to say next?

'Hello?'

'Hey. Yeah...I'm still here.'

'Well, how the hell are you?'

'It's Matt...' Her groan is audible on the other side of the phone, and her breath hitches while she waits for the news. If only it was something simple... 'Suicide.' The word is too soft on my tongue, it melts like something sweet. 'He tried to kill himself.' The consonants give it the hard edge that it deserves.

'What the fuck? Sarah, where are you?'

My lungs collapse inside my chest and at once I'm struggling to breathe. My throat hurts with the effort of heaving, bile rising from my stomach. 'Park.' Mumbling from behind my fingers, cupped as I try to gather air.

'Where?' Lisa's teeth make a clattering noise in my ear.

'Meadows. At the Meadows.'

'The one along from Summer Hall? At my end?'

Pause while I nod, and it's only when she doesn't say anything that I realise I have to speak, 'Yeah.'

'Fucking hell.' Cursing me? Herself? The situation? What situation? My chest rises and falls heavily, desperate to billow air. I don't remember why I called her in the first place.

'That fucking wanker. What a selfish piece of shit.' Lisa places a mug of something that clatters on the glass coffee table and brown oozes down the edge. Hot chocolate. The room is warm and bright. Lisa's flat is always warm and bright. Clutching at a cushion, blinking at the fairy lights surrounding the faux fireplace. My fingers are picking at thread; someone has sewn their own image on the cushion cover, but what is it supposed to be?

'I'm sorry. I'm sorry. He's your boyfriend and he loves you. I know that. But what the fucking hell? You're not supposed to go slashing your wrists if you're in love. Why? That doesn't even make sense.'

Shaking my head, my hair nearly falls into the mug as I lean over the steam, glad to feel the heat on my face. Glad to feel... 'It's not his fault.'

'Don't even think that it might have anything to do with you. Don't you dare.' Lisa's storming up and down the Persian rug in polka dot slippers, her face a livid red.

Do I sink into the sofa? Defend Matt? An inkling that something should happen, that I'm supposed to say something. But my fingernails are still just picking at the thread. My hands look ridiculous, worrying at a cross-stitch pattern while I do nothing else. Just fingers and thread. That's all that's left.

'If I was better, if I knew what to do....' Head still bent, but I can see the toes of Lisa's slippers. I don't have to look up to know that she's standing with her hands on her hips. I wonder if she uses that stance on the kids at the nursery. It must work.

'Sarah, the boy tried to kill himself. There's no knowing what was going through that stupid brain of his. That far gone, and there's no way he's been thinking straight.'

'But there must have been something -'

'What are you, a psychologist now? An expert?'

'No, but I loved him, and I should have known.' The words fall out of my mouth before I realise, and the sentence dangles awkwardly, invisible but strange.

Lisa sighs gently and moves to sit down next to me. 'Sarah, none of this is your fault. You love him, and that's as much as you could be expected to do. He made a stupid, stupid mistake, and he's an absolute fucker for letting that happen when he did. But listen, he's still alive and it's up to you what happens next. Don't let this hold you back, or I'll kill him myself.'

I can hear the warmth in her words, and on the arm she's moving around my hunched shoulders. 'I just want everything to be good again.' And when my sigh shudders, I see Matt smiling beneath a climbing frame, or kissing me in the shower, holding my hand on Princes Street, or handing me a card over a board game. 'I miss him.'

'I know.' Lisa stands, done with the sentiment now that she's able to give. Practically minded, and she's lifting a throw off the other sofa, 'Now you need to get yourself some rest and a proper sleep. Then you can think about what you want to do.'

Like it's my decision that I'm capable of making. I nod and sip carefully at the lukewarm chocolate. My head is full of nothing, and notion of sleep excites me. 'Thanks, for being so patient.'

'Hey,' she smiles and tosses a small pillow at my side, 'it's what I'm here for.'

They say that the church is the people, not the building, but standing beneath the stone-arch doorway the presence of God feels stronger than it has in years. A kindly old woman offers me an order of service and I take it gratefully from her, nodding my thanks in that silent but friendly way so often found in churches. It's still cold inside, the congregation clutching tightly at their coats, readjusting their scarves to get the full benefit, keeping their singing voices warm. The pews towards the back are more appealing to me, especially as it means I don't have to walk the full length of the aisle, painfully aware that an unknown youth is something of a mystery among the elders and the elderly. Gossiping grannies and grumbling granddads pause in their disapproving conversations and they accept that they'll have to continue over tea and stale biscuits after the sermon. Heavy organ droning reverberates across the tiled floor, filling the crevices of the old brick walls before drowning us, resting along thick wooden beams. My eyes trace the shape of the church before I notice the man standing by the table. He is younger than my prejudiced notions would have believed and over his black robes he wears a long scarf, decorated with flowers and crosses and Latin. Rich in greens and purples.

What can he tell me of salvation and forgiveness? I need him to set everything straight, to read words from the Bible that make instant sense. Why our heads are broken, why his arms are cut, why love really isn't enough.

THIRTY

Matt

White. The infamous colour of death - the flashes, the light, the pearly gates. Here white is the shade of purgatory, a place where everything's in transit - coming and going, going and coming. There are walls here, and they are white. There are sheets on the bed, and they are white.

Colour is present in the shape of Sarah. She is red boots, blue dress, brown hair, yellow ribbon. Sarah carries a rainbow in her arms, a collection of flowers never found in nature, too beautiful to be real. Primrose, she calls them. And hyacinth. Tulips. She unwraps the bouquet, cellophane wrap crisping through the silence of the room. Pink ribbons and curls are tied around the vase. Prepared, she takes a small set of scissors from her bag, cutting the stems and releasing a scent of green.

'Sarah...' Lying on his back, spine sunk into the mattress, face burying into the pillow; Matt watches her. He knew she was coming, just from the sound that her boots made against the hospital floor.

'You're awake.' Is all she says, a tone heavy with meaning despite the scarcity of words.

'Where did you go?' His voice is firm, his larynx the only

part that hasn't been damaged in his attempts. Matt's chest heaves, pregnant with breath that is leaden with sentiment. But it escapes only in a sigh.

She's not looking at him, lingering by the guest chair at the side of the bed. Moments pass and she allows herself to drop, the objects of her handbag clattering together as she sits. Keys, phone, make-up, iPod, Polo mints. Matt knows they're all always in there.

'I didn't want to kill myself.' A ridiculous line, pathetic in all that it means. Suicide isn't easy, and it sure as hell is painless. Not that way - not with a razor blade poised above skin, not when the edge slices through flesh, not when the blood blossoms from beneath the cracks.

Silence floods between them, an awkward space of thoughts left unsaid.

'I just wanted help.' Matt struggles on his bed, sitting himself up with the use of only one arm. The opposite lies useless on his lap, tightly wrapped in gauze.

'Matt.' Sarah breathes his name, like somehow she can communicate all feeling in just four letters. And she almost does. The final 't' clips his name short, causing Matt to focus his blurred attention on her face. In response, he wants to say everything and nothing, mentally bound by the hospital bed.

'I just...couldn't be here.'

'So you dumped me here and left?' Matt's words get caught in his throat, stuck behind his Adam's apple. His eyes brim with hot, heavy tears, heart pulling between anger and disappointment. There's something worse there too, something he's struggling to place his shaky finger on.

'I didn't know *what* to do, Matt. I couldn't just sit here, waiting -'

'No one asked you to do that.'

'So what *did* you want?'

'Visit me, be with me, I don't know, just love me.' Matt's response is immediate. It comes first from the heart, but his head follows soon after, checking Matt for his loaded requests.

'Stay? Why should I stay?' Sarah rises from her seat, knuckles white as she wrings her hands together. What is she grasping for? 'Matt, you just tried to *kill* yourself. After all.. After ev-er-y-thing. After I've tried so, so hard.'

'You think I didn't try, Sarah? Think I didn't try to live, try to want to live?'

A nurse shuffles by the door, his smile pleasant but his eyes cautiously flicking between patient and visitor.

'Is everything okay in here?'

Sarah's embarrassed by her outburst, turning her back to the door and pressing her forehead to the window pane.

'We're fine,' Matt says, his smile so practised it's close to authentic.

'Okay.' The nurse reveals his profile, addressing Sarah's back.

'He needs his rest. If you could keep your conversation calmer...' He pads down the corridor, the rest of his sentence going with him.

An ugly silence fills the room, penetrating through flesh and skull. So much is communicated by what is left unsaid. But unlike before there's no physicality - no touches or kisses that say 'Here I am. We're present. Life goes on.'

Matt sinks back into his hospital bed, glancing at the non-committal cards on the bed stand. "Get Well Soon" write Dan and Sue; not even a heart-felt message, just two names scribbled in necessity.

'Can't you forgive me?' Matt's throat croaks the words, giving a pathetic quality to his question, embarrassing.

'What part are you asking me to forgive?'

Matt turns to watch as Sarah's breath flowers the window with white clouds. He doesn't know.

'Maybe the part where I bled all over your grandparents' tiles? Or maybe the part where I didn't take my meds. Or, I don't know, maybe the part where my fucked up brain was diseased in the first place?' He almost wants to say more, wants to leave her with a bitter taste, but he bites his tongue, literally pressing it between his back teeth.

'Like none of this is your fault...' Anger slips into Sarah's tone, helpless hands clenching into fists by her side. As she turns, she raises them to her head, clutching at clumps of her hair, hair that is still so soft, and casting a warm brown glow about her head.

In better times, better places, Matt knows he would have risen from the bed, hidden her in his arms. She would stroke at the hair of his forearms while they shared a view from the window.

But though the space between them is only that of the small room, Matt sees Sarah as elusive: an intangible and impossible past.

'None of this *is* my fault. Think I *chose* to be here? Think I want to be prodded and poked and questioned? I'm mentally ill, for fuck's sake, not here out of curiosity.'

'But what did you ever do to stop it?' Accusation burns in Sarah's eyes; they seem red somehow...different.

'Everything.'

Blood is racing hot through Matt's system, the veins in his wrist pumping hard. Fear rises from his feet and into his lungs, breathing loathing, circulating hate. A dim voice in this back of his mind, by the nape of his neck, is warning him, but his blood is running thicker than his thoughts. The vase is made of plastic, the sharpest object the edge of the Hallmark Get Well Soon, there's nothing here but pillows and sheets and hands, hands smack against his jaw, slap hard against his cheek; the only weapon against himself is himself.

Sarah's at the bedside, grabbing Matt's wrists in her hands, holding them away from his face without applying too much pressure.

Matt's body gives up, flops backwards in defeat, and Sarah lets his arms drop at his side. His leg trembles; gentle tremors shaking the metal bed frame.

'Ssh...' Sarah's lips by his ear, a finger tentatively stroking at his temple. With a hand placed lightly on his chest, Sarah feels Matt's heart thudding at twice the tempo.

'Do you honestly think that I'd just let myself wind up here?' Matt's free to whisper, his voice soft against her jaw line. 'I have tried everything, Sarah. I've been to hell and back trying..' The back of his eyes prick with heat, the tears blurring his vision are painful. Sounds are stuck in his throat, surfacing as chokes and breathless splutters.

'I know, Matt, I know.' He can't be sure he's really hearing her, or if she's even speaking at all. Imagined or otherwise, the words soothe and slow the beating of his heart.

'I always tried my best.'

'I know, Matt, I know.'

Matt's head rocks gently left to right, salty tears sliding down his nose to rest on cracked lips, they taste almost dirty.

'But my trying's never good enough. I'm exhausted, Sarah. So tired...'

Footsteps shuffle slowly, retreating from his space. It's darkness until he opens his eyes, all light and furry shapes until his sight can focus. There is a chair. The chair is empty. A flash of colour by the door, then it's gone. There is a room, a bed, and Matt.

'Sarah!'

Matt's voice struggles, Matt's body is heavy. 'Sarah! ...Sarah...Say-' Matt's head and heart are Sarah.

THIRTY-ONE

Sarah

My name, he's calling my name, but I can't go back. Not now. It seems to echo down the corridor, and I drown out the sound with my fingers in my ears. My handbag clatters and it's only when I'm on the floor scooping up the contents that I realise that I squealed. Nurses pause, like they might ask if I'm okay, wondering if I'm a crazy patient too. A hand reaches in front of me and I take it – but it's not Matt. It's Johnny.

'Sarah, you alright?'

'I...just dropped my bag.' But I know that I'm shaking, struggling with the zip on my bag.

'How is he today?'

'He's awake...and –' And I don't know what else to say.

'Okay. You in again tomorrow?'

'I don't think so.'

'What?' Johnny, tilting his head, looking past me, failing to understand how anything can be more important than his best friend.

'I probably won't be back. For a while.'

'What are you talking about? You're his best chance of a cure. I mean, you're the only thing keeping him holding on. Please, you need to be here.'

But I was there, and still he couldn't hold on. I only realise I'm biting my nails when the red polish flakes between my teeth. I pick the ruby colour from my lips and don't know what to do with it, so I wipe my hands down my thighs. 'I can't.' I'm not sure exactly what it is that I can't, but the feeling is crushing inside me somewhere, that irrepressible *cannot.*

'I wouldn't spout this crap if I didn't really mean it. You're his whole life by now. That boy needs you. Seriously.'

'But what about what *I* need?' I teeter, feeling my heels wobble, like they're ready to collapse under a great weight.

Johnny scratches the back of his head and inspects his nails, frowning, 'All I'm saying is that you guys should work it out. Before you, I've never seen him so happy.'

Happy? A scream is urging up from the bottom of my throat but turns into a noise I don't recognise, 'You call that happy? Tubes and supervision and extra skin grafts?' That look in Johnny's eyes says it better; I feel like that much sorrow. 'I'm sorry...but I've tried. So hard.' The sobbing is hard enough that I have to hold my stomach, and Johnny is blurred but closer, placing a hand on my shoulder.

'Sarah, we all try. It's not easy -'

I shake my head and tears splash off the end of my nose. 'I'm out of trying. I'm tired. So tired.' My bones are beyond exhausted, I can feel them shaking. My body sags and all I want is to crumble into the floor. Johnny's fingers squeeze into my shoulder, and the pain makes me move away.

I press a finger beneath each eye, careful not to let my eyeliner run. I have to get out this hospital, and I have to leave the same woman I was when I came in: collected, composed, and sure that she has a place in the world. Where and what is anybody's bet. But alive, and stepping through the hospital doors. A spitting rain, a sun trying hard to spread its rays through the clouds.

'Hey,' Lisa pushes herself away from the wall, crushing the end of her cigarette beneath her boot. She smiles and it's real. 'You okay?'

'Do I look okay?' My lips feel lopsided in their attempt at a smile, and Lisa wraps her arms around me carefully, like I'm fragile, breakable.

'You look great. And you'll feel great soon too. I promise.'

And I will, because I haven't broken.

I turn and look at the rows of identical windows. Any could belong to Matt. Or maybe none of them do. But I look, and I wish Matt to know that I'm looking, and seeing. I close my eyes, and want to run inside, and lay myself next to him, share his bed and his warmth, whisper that I'll make everything better.

But he has to wake up. He has to do that for him, and I'll do that for me. Maybe then.

'Sarah, the bus is here. Are you ready?'

'I'm ready.'

About the author

Bethany Ruth Anderson was born in Falkirk twenty six years ago. Since then she has scribbled many short stories and poems, and graduated with an MLitt in Creative Writing from the University of Glasgow. Bethany currently lives in Edinburgh, where she works as a high school English teacher. *Swings and Roundabouts* is her first novel.

You can find her on Twitter @subtlemelodrama

Bamboccioni Books

bamboccioni n.
1. *plural form of* bamboccione, *meaning an overgrown baby or mama's boy.*

Established in 2010, **Bamboccioni Books** is a small and independent publisher. We specialise in high quality fiction and aim to promote new and diverse writers. We are particularly dedicated to publishing short stories and niche fiction that would be otherwise overlooked by larger publishers.

For more information and to keep up to date with our latest news, please visit our website:

www.bamboccionibooks.com